4J
RB
2C

"You're quite a woman, Lisa."

Tray continued. "You deserve more than...than this," he said, his gesture taking in the kitchen. "We have to decide where we go from here."

"We?" Lisa blinked. "I don't know about you, but I am very well prepared to take care of myself."

"You've proved that. But we both know this is temporary. I might be able to make you an offer...."

D1622732

Eva Rutland began writing when her four children, now all successful professionals, were growing up. Eva lives in California with her husband, Bill, who actively supports and encourages her writing career.

Books by Eva Rutland

HARLEQUIN ROMANCE®
3439—MARRIAGE BAIT
3490—THE WEDDING TRAP
3518—THE MILLION-DOLLAR MARRIAGE
3550—HER OWN PRINCE CHARMING

Don't miss any of our special offers. Write to us at the following address for information on our newest releases.

Harlequin Reader Service
U.S.: 3010 Walden Ave., P.O. Box 1325, Buffalo, NY 14269
Canadian: P.O. Box 609, Fort Erie, Ont. L2A 5X3

ALMOST A WIFE
Eva Rutland

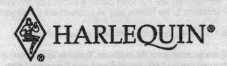

HARLEQUIN®

TORONTO • NEW YORK • LONDON
AMSTERDAM • PARIS • SYDNEY • HAMBURG
STOCKHOLM • ATHENS • TOKYO • MILAN • MADRID
PRAGUE • WARSAW • BUDAPEST • AUCKLAND

If you purchased this book without a cover you should be aware
that this book is stolen property. It was reported as "unsold and
destroyed" to the publisher, and neither the author nor the
publisher has received any payment for this "stripped book."

With love, to my delightful granddaughter,
Chelsea, and her bear.

ISBN 0-373-03621-3

ALMOST A WIFE

First North American Publication 2000.

Copyright © 2000 by Eva Rutland.

All rights reserved. Except for use in any review, the reproduction or
utilization of this work in whole or in part in any form by any electronic,
mechanical or other means, now known or hereafter invented, including
xerography, photocopying and recording, or in any information storage
or retrieval system, is forbidden without the written permission of the
publisher, Harlequin Enterprises Limited, 225 Duncan Mill Road,
Don Mills, Ontario, Canada M3B 3K9.

All characters in this book have no existence outside the imagination of
the author and have no relation whatsoever to anyone bearing the same
name or names. They are not even distantly inspired by any individual
known or unknown to the author, and all incidents are pure invention.

This edition published by arrangement with Harlequin Books S.A.

® and TM are trademarks of the publisher. Trademarks indicated with
® are registered in the United States Patent and Trademark Office, the
Canadian Trade Marks Office and in other countries.

Visit us at www.eHarlequin.com

Printed in U.S.A.

PROLOGUE

LISA REYNOLDS gazed with apprehension at the empty lobby of the Bonus Bank Building. No one standing by the bank of elevators. No telling when someone would come and choose the one marked Floors 21 to 40.

She walked to that elevator, and courageously lifted her finger.

She couldn't push the button.

This was crazy! Just because it happened once didn't mean you were going to be stuck every time you stepped into an elevator.

She wasn't crazy. Hadn't she breezed through college, and earned a master's degree in business by the time she was twenty-three! Now, at twenty-six, she was director of research and development at CTI—Computer Technology Incorporated.

Not anymore, she reminded herself.

Well, she hadn't lost the job because she wasn't darn good at it.

Mergers! That was what was crazy. All these takeover, downsizing shenanigans going on in business today.

Anyway, it was CTI's loss, not hers. She already had feelers out. With her qualifications, she'd be hired by the competition in a hot minute.

Maybe with an office on the ground floor, she

thought, trying to laugh at herself. Why couldn't she lose this ridiculous phobia about elevators!

She had almost overcome it. Out of necessity. She could hardly have climbed the stairs to her thirty-fourth floor office each working day for one whole year. She had compromised. She would board the elevator only if someone got on with her. That way she wouldn't be alone in death or disaster.

She should have come earlier. Not everybody had lost their job, and the elevators would have been crowded with workers.

Bad timing. Stupid to think being a little late didn't matter because it was her last day.

She straightened hopefully as a woman breezed into the lobby. But the woman stopped at the one to twenty-block. Lisa stepped back as if waiting for someone. She pretended to be studying the mural on the opposite wall while gazing surreptitiously at the woman. She looked very chic in a smart gabardine business suit, one leather gloved hand clutching a smart leather attaché case.

Like me, Lisa thought, touching a hand to the cloud of silky black hair that framed her face in a smart shoulder-length cut. I'm coiffured, manicured and groomed as sleek as the sleekest of women executives! And I'm more efficient than most. Sam Fraser said so.

"I hate doing this to you," he had said when he handed her the pink slip that terminated her employment. "Research and development was gaining momentum under your management, and it's not your fault that we've dropped in the market."

"But that's only temporary," she protested, at the

moment more concerned with the potential of CTI's software than with her personal problem. "Of course we show a slump in the market when a large share of funds is going into development. But when the new programs are on the market, our stock will go up."

"Yeah," Sam agreed. "But the merger hangs on the current rating. Tray Kingsley, the man who's negotiating the deal, is looking at the market and if our stock doesn't go up, a sell-off will begin. We've got to cut overhead to raise profit. Middle management is the first to go. Sorry."

So her job had vanished. Just like that. Just because some big shot sat in his New York office, studying the stock market. A big shot named Tray Kingsley. She hadn't known she could hate a man she'd never seen.

What could he tell about the real worth of CTI, sitting on his backside three thousand miles away?

More to the point…why the dickens did CTI decide to merge with Lawson Enterprises just at this time! She had been with them only one year, hardly eligible for the golden handshake!

She straightened again as a man entered the building. Any other time she might have noticed that he was tall, dark and quite handsome. But this morning she only noticed that he headed straight for the 21 to 40 block of elevators. She sprang into action.

Tray Kingsley smiled as he pushed the button. He was on the way up in more ways than one. After only one year with Lawson, he had been chosen to negotiate the takeover of CTI, for which he had re-

ceived a sizable bonus. Now he had been selected
as the new CEO to head the new San Francisco sub-
sidiary. His tenure here was only temporary, an opportunity to study the facility and decide the best
economic shifts. But the bonus included a substan-
tial increase in salary, and a brief taste of sunny
California. You couldn't beat that with a stick.

Actually he had suggested the California stint
himself. It provided a diplomatic breather from his
indecisive involvement with a very persistent lady
who just happened to be the boss's daughter.

Not much of a breather. He still maintained his
position at the New York headquarters and would
be there often. And, to be fair, he enjoyed his as-
sociation with Chase Lawson. She was beautiful,
and charmingly acquainted with all the right people,
a companionable asset in any social gathering.
Personally? He tried to think beyond the social
swirls to the little dinners and their intimate times
alone. Well… Perhaps the fact that she was a
Lawson was the put off. He liked to think his ad-
vancement was due to his capabilities…not as a future son-in-law.

So, back to the job, he thought as the elevator
door slid open. This would be his first look at the
physical site, but he was already immersed in plans
for improvement and expansion. The first thing to
do was—

"Pardon," he said, a little startled and not sure
who had brushed against whom, for they seemed to
enter the elevator simultaneously. He didn't look at
her, and hardly noticed that there was no response.

The key man here was Sam Fraser, he thought.

Perhaps he could arrange to take him to lunch. Talking was better than looking when it came to sizing things up. He meant to get a good grip on things right off. Wouldn't bother about an apartment. The hotel was convenient and...

"Oh, my God!" The heartrending wail commanded his full attention.

What the hell!

He turned to see the woman crouching in terror, the wail escalating into a crescendo of uncontrollable sobs.

He bent toward her. "What...what is it?"

"We're stuck. We're stuck. Oh, my God! I knew it. I knew this would happen! Oh, God, oh God, oh God!"

Her hysteria was so unnerving, it was a moment before he realized she was right. The elevator had stopped somewhere between floors. He was about to sound the alarm, but she blocked his way.

"I shouldn't have got in...I wish I hadn't. I wish I hadn't."

He wished so, too. She was losing it. He tried to reassure her. "Hey, it's okay. I'll alert somebody." Whoever's in charge of the damn thing...if she'll shut up!

He shook her gently, and tried to cut into the now incoherent babble. "Hush. It will be all right."

The mass of black hair swung around her face as she violently shook her head. He couldn't tell whether she was laughing or crying.

Clearly hysterical. He didn't want to slap her. If he kissed her?

His mouth closed on hers, shutting off the

screams. Or shocked her into silence. For... Good Lord! The kiss was more potent than a slap. Her soft yielding surprised him, evoking an exciting erotic spasm of... What on earth was he doing!

He tried to release her, but he couldn't.

She clung to the feeling. His arms around her, secure and warm. Safe.

The pressure of his lips against hers...demanding, teasing, pleading. Her whole body responded, awakening to a strange exhilarating sensation of desire that pleased and held her.

Each time he tried to pull away, her grip tightened. Her head was buried on his shoulder and an alluring scent of fresh shampoo mixed with an exotic perfume wafted from the hair covering his chest. Her arms held him close. Too close. A hell of a time for the way she was making him feel!

With an effort, he took control. At least he had shut her up.

Over her shoulder he reached for the phone connected to the alarm.

She heard him on the phone. "Hello, hello... Is anybody there?"

Her head jerked up as the panic returned. She still held him tight, but she vehemently declared, "No! Nobody. They won't come... Oh, God! Oh, God!"

Hell, she was off again and whoever was supposed to answer the alarm was out to lunch! "Shut up!" he shouted. He felt tears dampening his shirt and softened his tone, "I can't hear if you're not quiet. Just be patient. They'll have us out of here in a jiffy."

"They won't. We were stuck for almost two hours!"

"Oh? It happened before?" This elevator must be a jinx. But it should have been fixed. "When?" he asked.

"Two years ago. At my old apartment. But there were only seven stories," she said. "We were stuck halfway to third and we had to climb out."

"Oh." Her apartment. It wasn't this elevator. The woman was the jinx. The thought made him laugh.

That seemed to make her mad. Not mad enough to turn him loose, but she flared up at him. "Why are you laughing? It's not funny. Do you realize we're stuck between no telling how many stories of solid wall? This elevator doesn't stop until the twenty-first floor. No way to climb out like we did... That is, if something doesn't break loose and we go crashing to the ground. That time at my apartment, we decided that if that happened, we would jump up and down so when it hit, we—"

"Hey! That's enough." Hysteria was better than her crazy predictions. She was making him nervous. Still...best to keep her talking.. "You may be an old hand at this, but you're not an expert. Elevators have springs on the bottom, so if they hit bottom, it's not with a crash."

"Oh?" She looked up at him, eyes wide. "Is that true?"

He nodded, though he wasn't sure. He also wondered about all that solid wall between openings. He pushed the alarm, and spoke again into the phone. "Hello. Anybody there?"

"They weren't when we called," she said. "We'd

probably have been there all night if it hadn't been for the pizza.''

"Pizza?''

"A girl on the elevator was delivering a pizza, and this guy on four came to see why she hadn't gotten there, and found out the elevator was stuck. If he hadn't, we might have been…'' She stopped, struck by another alarming thought. "Maybe it's an earthquake.''

"Earthquake?''

"They told us never to use the elevator during an earthquake. They cut off the electricity you know, and—''

"If there was an earthquake, you'd damn well feel it,'' he snapped. "And if the electricity was off this phone wouldn't be—'' A voice on the other end stopped him. A reassuring voice. He smiled. "Oh. Sure. Okay.'' He looked down at her. "It's okay. Be calm. Help is on the way.''

She didn't release him until the elevator started its ascent. Then she moved, turning away from him, mopping at her tear stained face.

"Sorry I was such a nuisance. Thank you,'' she said, and bolted as soon as the elevator came to a smooth stop at the thirty-fourth floor.

He was straightening his tie, and only nodded. When he stepped out of the elevator, she had disappeared.

CHAPTER ONE

"SO YOU got stuck in the elevator!" Mike said.

"It's not funny," Lisa scolded, but she laughed with him. At least he didn't know she had acted like an idiot.

"Well, you're only a little late," he said, and pushed open the door of the conference room.

Lisa gasped. Looking at all the gang, waiting to say goodbye, at the table laden with goodies and gifts, made her all teary. She didn't want that.

"What's this! You're celebrating my getting canned?"

"Sure thing." Mike grinned. "I warned you. Squash my creative talents one more time and you were out of here!"

"Stingy with the supplies, too. Slow," Jim said. "Took me all of two days to get those bytes I needed."

Others joined in the bashing, and the laughter made it easier. Not much easier. She really hated leaving…right in the midst of everything it seemed. Things changed fast in softwear, and you had to be on the ball to get there first. And they were getting there, for instance what Mike was developing with—

"Stop it, you guys! Come on, Lisa." Pam, who was fashioning a special keyboard that was bound to be a major success, led her to the table. "Help yourself. Coffee?"

13

Lisa nodded and smiled at the Japanese girl she had hired only a few short months before. One of the three new people she had hired after convincing the head office that if they were to capture the international market, they had to offer a keyboard and program compatible with the nuances of the different languages. But now that she was leaving...

Egotist! You think you're the whole kit and caboodle, that the wheels of progress stop with your departure? These are the scientists and technicians. You were just one spoke in the wheel.

An important spoke, she told herself with a touch of bitterness. I dealt with the idiosyncracies of this talented crew, I was the mediator between them and management, I fought for their ideas, got the supplies, monitored the deadlines, and—

"I brought champagne," Mike said.

"And I baked the cake," Linda said.

"I thank you both. My favorite drink, and my favorite cake," she said, forcing a jocular mood. She sure wasn't going to spoil the goodbye party they had planned. "You guys go easy on these goodies. What's left goes home with me,"

"Stashing, huh?"

"Sure. No telling how long before another paycheck." Lisa laughed with them. There was another job out there waiting for her, and she'd find it. She wasn't worried, and the good mood held.

At the end of the day, as she approached the elevator, she felt the familiar prickles of panic, more pronounced because of the morning's episode. The champagne may have bolstered her. Anyway, several others were risking the downward plunge so, despite the mounting trepidation, she managed to board with them.

She shut her eyes, remembering, feeling the claustrophobia and imminent danger of crashing or being forever trapped. The warmth and security of a man's arms around her, the gentleness. The shock of sheer pleasure when his lips touched hers. She wished...

No she didn't! She had acted like an idiot! Better never to see him again in life.

They had reached the lobby, and the doors slid open giving her a feeling of overwhelming relief as she walked away from the enclosed cubicle.

Everything happens for the best, she thought. She'd make sure her next office was on the ground floor.

From the bank building, she turned right to traverse the few short blocks to her apartment near the wharf. She liked her apartment. A one bedroom, but the bath was big with a separate dressing area, and the living-room space was large with lush carpeting. She had carefully chosen one on the bottom floor and found it offered more than just *no elevator*. Easy access to the community exercise room, laundry room and swimming pool. She meant to keep it.

If she could.

It wasn't cheap. That hadn't bothered her in the least when she left her so-so job in Sacramento to move to San Francisco to take the job with CTI. The enormous salary was a godsend. Not only could she afford the apartment, but she could help finance her grandparents' move to the Sprightly Seniors retirement complex.

When she was five years old, her parents had been killed in an automobile crash, and she had moved in with her grandparents. Their love enclosed her, a warm blanket that bolstered the shock...she, from the loss of both parents, and they from the loss of an only daughter. She had basked in that love, attention, things, for they had denied her nothing. Hers had been a privileged world, and she had danced her way through it...the private schools, music and dancing lessons, swimming, skiing, family vacations in Europe. She had never even been burdened with domestic chores, for they always had household help. Her grandmother had never worked outside the house, but remained at home to care for Lisa and enjoy her clubs and social functions. Her grandfather had only been a high school principal, but...

No wonder she had thought they were rich!

She found out they weren't when Gramps retired, and decided they should buy into the senior citizens complex where many of their friends were already living.

"If we can swing it," he had said.

For the first time she became aware of their financial status. She discovered that their style of living had strained Grandpa's salary to the hilt, and their modest home had been heavily mortgaged to finance Lisa's stint at Stanford. However, proceeds from the sale of the house and their few investments made it possible to buy a two-bedroom apartment in the senior complex.

Lisa, who was just starting the job in San Francisco, was happy to see them so comfortably settled. The monthly maintenance fee included three meals a day, cleaning services and an abundance of recreational and social features, as well as continuing life care.

The thing was, Gramps's monthly pension check barely covered the cost of all these benefits. Lisa, feeling quite wealthy with her new salary, supplemented with a sizable sum every month. Gramps had protested, but she insisted. She had been glad to supply the extra, happy that she could repay in some small measure all they had given to her.

But now...

Lisa felt the first small prickle of alarm. She had been walking on air. She had splurged on everything—apartment, furnishings, clothes, you name it.

One year ago. And now the job and big money were gone. Swish!

Even if she gave up the apartment, what would she do with all that unpaid for furniture? That was another thing. Bills.

The city was alive now. People pouring out of buildings and filling the sidewalks, bumper-to-bumper traffic. Lisa hardly noticed as she dodged other pedestrians and kept to her usual brisk pace, mentally calculating.

How did the saying go? Like father...like son? No, in this sexist era, it would be mother/daughter. She chuckled. Like her grandparents, she'd been living it up to the hilt. She had given little thought to saving and, with her usual high lifestyle, she barely made it from payday to payday.

She had one paycheck and one month's severance pay. No more. She'd have to find another job quick.

Again she reminded herself that she wasn't worried. She had already put in some applications listing her credentials, experience and excellent references from Sam. She was well qualified. The possibilities were endless.

Tomorrow she had an appointment with the Corry Corporation, and she had two interviews scheduled next week. All looked pretty promising, just a matter of choice. She felt very confident as she shed her clothes and headed for the swimming pool.

Three weeks later, she did not feel so confident as she faced Mr. Brown of Safe Securities, the last company on her list.

"Your qualifications are excellent, Ms. Reynolds, and I would like very much to have you aboard, but..." He paused, nervously shuffling papers on his desk. Probably the papers containing proof of her excellent qualifications, she thought with irony. "As I said, at the present time, we are cutting back, not hiring."

Same story she had heard from others. Why was everybody downsizing at the same time?

"I can't promise anything, but, in a few months, our position might be different." He went on, again praising her credentials.

He was trying to let her down easily. She helped him out. "I do understand, Mr. Brown. And thank you for taking the time to explain the situation." She managed to make a graceful exit, and soon was outside his office, in the corridor.

The empty corridor. Wasn't anybody going down?

Probably not. Long after lunchtime, long before quitting time.

Oh, for goodness' sake! Of course she could get in an elevator by herself!

She walked toward it. Hesitated.

Started to punch the button. Didn't push it.

She'd feel pretty foolish if someone walked down the hall and saw her just standing there...headed neither up or down. This paranoia about elevators was not only silly, it was darn inconvenient!

But... Didn't everything come in threes? That time at her old apartment, then three weeks ago at the bank...

Well, only five stories. Her smart pumps had low heels and she had plenty of time. She found the stairwell, swung through the door and started down. The exercise would be good for her legs.

She had plenty of time to think as she made her way down, step by step. She'd check the want ads more carefully, though it appeared to be nothing in her line there.

What was her line anyway?

Business, of course! She had her MBA to prove it. Training, experience.

Okay! Okay! Where does that get you if there are no job openings! Maybe she should get on the list of some employment agency, sign up for one of those job placement seminars. Do something, or pretty soon she'd have to put in for unemployment benefits. She hadn't bothered to do that because she'd thought by now that something would have turned up.

Good, At last she was on the first floor. Gratefully she reached for the door.

It didn't budge.

She shook it, but it held fast.

First floor. Security? No access unless you had business.

That was stupid. That bank of elevators was plenty accessible to anyone.

Well... Someone had to come near that stairwell sooner or later, and she would bang on that door until somebody heard her.

Ten minutes later, the door was opened by a woman in a chic tan coatdress, a smart leather purse slung over her shoulder. She shook back her sheath of smooth blond hair and stared at Lisa. "What were you doing in there?"

Lisa touched a finger to her own sleekly cropped hair, adjusted her own smart shoulder bag. "Thought I'd walk down for the exercise. A big mistake. I didn't know they locked this door."

"In some buildings. For security I think."

"Funny kind of security. Anyway, thank you for letting me out. I could have been there forever," she said, smiling as she walked away, head and shoulders high.

When she reached her apartment, and opened the door, she heard the vacuum cleaner humming.

Joline. Her weekly cleaning lady, one of the splurges that accompanied the big salary. Oh, she had felt so grand. No more scrubbing tiles, changing linens, dusting. All she had to do was water her plants, and arrange fresh flowers when the gang was coming over or she had a date.

Well, she wouldn't be having a gang over anytime soon. Most were from work, and she had another agenda now. And Chris, the guy in accounting that she'd been dating, had transferred to Seattle three months ago. He must have seen the downsizing coming.

At any rate, she'd have to do her own cleaning now. She'd put off telling Joline because she'd been so sure she'd have another job by this time. Now...

She deserved notice, too, didn't she? Two weeks? A month?

"Come and have a cup of coffee with me, Joline," she said when the woman had finished her chores. "I'm afraid I have a bit of bad news for you. For me, anyway."

"Thank you. I could do with a cup of coffee, and I'm glad to take a load off my feet for a spell." Joline, who was rather heavy, settled herself in a chair by the coffee table. "But...bad news? I don't like the sound of that."

"I don't like it, either," Lisa said, as she poured coffee. "I hate to say it, but I can't afford you any longer."

"Oh? I'm sorry. I like working here. You're not as messy as most."

She didn't ask why, but Lisa explained anyway.

Joline was sympathetic. "That's a shame. Goodness, I don't know what's happening these days. Mr. Taylor, on the fourth floor, gave me notice last month. He lost his job and had to take one in Lodi. Much less pay, he told me. Times are getting tough."

"Yes," Lisa said, thinking she might have to move to another area herself. She'd hate to leave the city, her nice apartment. Then another thought returned...notice. "Would two weeks notice be fair, Joline? Or would you prefer severance pay?"

"Oh, honey, you got enough problems. Don't worry about me."

"Are you sure?" Lisa was relieved, but she wanted to be fair.

"Sure I'm sure. I know how it is when you lose

a job. And, to tell the truth, I've got more than I need. I turned down three jobs just last week.''

"You did?" Lisa whistled. "No downsizing in the cleaning industry, huh?''

"You can say that again. And you can set your own pace, pick and choose.''

Lisa listened with idle curiosity as Joline elaborated. "You're your own boss, set your own wages. Like I charged old Mr. Jenkins double 'cause his place was a pigsty. And you can charge an arm and a leg out in the Heights and the Cove.''

"Oh?''

"Yeah. But you got to drive all the way out there, and you get plumb wore out climbing them stairs.''

"Stairs?''

"Oh, you know. All those Victorian houses got them winding stairs to the second floor. No. I couldn't stand that. Even if one house do pay more than three apartments. Mrs. Smith called me yesterday, trying to get me to come back. I told her no, *sirree,* not me.''

Lisa stared, her interest perked. Set your own pace. Your own price. An arm and a leg in the Heights with all those stairs... Stairs.

No elevators!

Anybody could clean a house.

She calculated. Set your own price? An arm and a leg?

Just temporary...while she was looking.

"Joline,'' she said. "Could you give me a reference?''

CHAPTER TWO

HE HADN'T seen her again. Not in the two months since he'd been at CTI.

That was strange. She got off on the same floor. Must work for the company.

Not necessarily. He'd been through every office, meeting the key people, assessing things, and he'd taken a careful, though cursory glance at every woman. He hadn't seen her. Not once.

Heck, he probably wouldn't recognize her. Her face had been buried in his shoulder most of the time.

If he knew her name, he'd ask... No, he wouldn't. Too wacky for his taste.

So why did she linger in his mind? At the strangest times. Even in his dreams...that mass of freshly shampooed hair, that faint scent of perfume, that soft yielding.

The ringing intruded.

The alarm. He stretched a hand to shut it off.

The ringing continued. The phone. He picked it up.

"Tray, darling! Did I wake you?"

"And how pleasant a wake up!" he managed to say, rousing from his stupor. "How are you, Chase?"

"Missing you. And worried about you. You're still stuck in that hotel."

23

"'Fraid so.''

"Poor baby. We'll have to do something about that.''

We? "I'm okay." What's with this *we?* Haven't reached that stage yet!

Okay, he'd been rather flattered when Chase Smith-Lawson centered her attention upon him. Recently divorced, she had returned to her father's palatial home, her maiden name and her role as leading hostess in New York's social set. She was the spoiled apple of her father's eye. She was also beautiful, glamorous, stimulating and... Face it. Officious!

"Tray, are you listening?"

"Sure. Trying to get a word in to tell you I want be here long enough to need an apartment."

Nonsense. "I knew you'd need me. I promised Daddy I'd be there to help you find the proper place, meet the proper people. Start you off on the right foot, so to speak."

That grated. Like his rapid rise at Lawson Enterprises wasn't due to his business acumen, but to his relationship with Lawson's daughter. "I think I'm getting my foot where it belongs. Into business, so to speak."

She missed the sarcasm. "I know. As always, you're probably working your head off in that stuffy office and still stuck in that stuffy hotel room. Don't worry. I'll get you out of both."

"Listen, Chase. I'm fine. I—"

She didn't hear him. "But not right away," she was saying. "Page Anderson wants me here to help with the Symphony Ball."

"Oh?" Thank God for Page Anderson.

"Can you manage without me for the next six weeks?"

"I'll try." He tried not to sound relieved. "I'll try."

Later that morning, Tray looked across his desk at Sam Fraser, who, in his two short months at CTI, had become his chief aide. "Okay, Sam, get ready. We're making some changes."

"What kind of changes?"

"Diversification." Anticipated changes that had been thrashed out at the corporate board meeting last week. "You must have expected it."

"Guess I did. Lots of relocations, huh?"

"Yes. Guess there will have to be. Each operation with its own specialty. That's Lawson policy. Production in Denver, research and development in—"

Fraser interrupted. "What's our role?"

Tray, noting his wary expression, smiled. "Don't worry. You're not moving. We're considering this as our marketing base. East coast, Asia and the Middle East, and you're my number one man. Quite a bit of travel, however. Is that a problem?"

"Not really. Not as big a problem as transplanting Sandy and the kids. Tim, the eldest, is at Cove High, basketball and all that stuff, and to take him away now would... Oh, you know how it is." He spread his hands. "So what's the procedure."

"Relocation. That's a first. If we—" His buzzer sounded and he picked it up. "Yes?"

"A Mr. Canson, sir, attorney at law, from Columbus, Ohio. He says it's urgent."

"Put him on," he said, wondering. "Canson? He didn't know a Canson. Nobody in Columbus but... "Tray Kingsley," he said into the phone. He listened, trying to absorb the shock, a creeping feeling of sorrow. Kathy Byrd dead. Sudden. A heart attack. "I am sorry." Vaguely he wondered why he had been called. "Is there anything I can do?"

He listened again, longer this time, astonished. "Of course," he finally said. "I understand." He didn't understand, but he added, "I'll be there as soon as possible."

At four that afternoon, he sat on a plane to Columbus, Ohio, still trying to understand. Trying to absorb the shock. Kathy Byrd dead. She was only... He added the years. Twenty-six. Strange. Same age Pete had been when he died two years ago.

Pete and Kathy Byrd. Both gone.

He stared out at the clouds, feeling a little numb. Of all the rotten luck.

He remembered the lawyer's words, "All of her affairs left in your hands. It has taken me some time to find you."

"Yes." He had moved twice in the two years since he had seen her. Despite the sorrow, he felt a bit of irritation. Why me?

And at this crucial time, just as he was about to get going with all these new developments. "I am sorry," he had said again, "I can't leave San Francisco at this time."

"Mr. Kingsley, it's imperative that you come immediately because of the children.'

That gave him pause. Poor little tykes...couldn't be quite out of the toddler stage. "Are they all right?" he had asked anxiously. "I mean, who's taking care of—?"

"A friend," the lawyer assured him. "They've been with her all week."

He felt relieved. Of course. Kathy would have long ago made some arrangement for the children in case of her death. She was that practical.

Absently he wondered what was his role. Probably executor to be sure her plans were carried out. She was not one to skip details. He had been amazed at how well she had dealt with Pete's death.

He had come then because she called him. Even though she had been surrounded by friends and neighbors, she had clung to him.

"You're family," she had said.

He had been touched, but they were not at all related. She had been just one in the gang that hung around his house during the growing up years in Dayton, Ohio. His had been that kind of house. His mother that kind of mother, he thought, and felt the familiar lump in his throat. She had been so loving, full of fun and easygoing, never minding the noise at the Ping-Pong table or around the basketball hoop that hung above the garage door the constant splashing of the swimming pool. Kids from the nearby Children's Home, Kathy and Pete among them, had been welcome and frequent visitors. Pete and he had been pretty close, same teams through Little and Pony League, same classes during high school. And

Kathy, always and forever Pete's girlfriend, had tagged along. The two of them had frequently double-dated with him and Gloria or whoever had been his current crush.

After high school, they had gone their separate ways. He went on to Harvard, and would probably have lost touch altogether, had it not been for his mother who was on the board of the Children's Home, and took a personal interest in several of the kids. She kept him informed. "Pete's waiting tables, and studying to be a court reporter...Kathy's working at the bank." He had come home to be best man at their wedding, and later, godfather for their first child. But then...his mother died.

For a moment he was back in that nightmare. She had had a heart attack and he returned home. Too late.

He shook off the feeling that always haunted him when he thought of his mother.

Anyway, Pete and Kathy moved to Columbus and, well, just faded into his past.

Until Pete died, and Kathy called. He had gone to Columbus then and found capable Kathy distraught and trying to cope, saddled as she was with a babe in arms and a three-year-old. Though grief-stricken, she had not been in bad shape financially, what with Pete's life and mortgage insurance. He had been doing well as a court reporter, with Kathy typing the transcripts at home. During his illness, she had begun transcribing for other court reporters, and was assured of a steady income. Tray had only needed to give solace as best he could, and help iron out the legal details concurrent with death. He had promised to stay in touch. "Call if you need me. Anytime for anything."

"Cocktail, sir?"

He looked up at the Flight attendant. "Whiskey and soda, please. Thanks," he said, taking a swallow before setting the glass on his tray. He needed it. He was assailed by guilt. He hadn't kept in touch.

Oh, a few phone calls in answer to her infrequent notes. Birthday and Christmas presents for the kids. But he hadn't been back, not once. He often went back to visit Dad, who was still working as a pharmacist, still living in Dayton, though he had moved from the old home to a condo, complete with golf course, swimming pool and cronies.

Dayton, he reminded himself, wasn't all that far from Columbus... But no, he hadn't kept in touch.

I'm in touch now, he thought, two days later, when he sat on a plane headed back to California. He was accompanied by a six-year-old girl holding tight to a teddy bear almost as big as she, and a four-year-old boy clutching a peppermint stick in very sticky fingers.

Quite a bundle for a bachelor accustomed to traveling light. Especially when the bundles were alive and kicking!

"No! I don't want this thing 'round me." The boy pushed at the seat belt with surprising strength.

"It's just till we get going," Tray apologized, desperately trying to get boy, girl and teddy bear buckled in.

"You have to, Peter." It was the girl who got the

boy's attention. "You know like Mommy always did in the car."

"I want Mommy!"

"Mommy's in heaven," the girl said, repeating as before, that Mommy was never coming back. It broke Tray's heart every time she said it. Her big blue eyes would grow even more solemn and sad. Not the happy child she had been when he had seen her two years ago.

"Her real name is Chelsea, but we call her Sunny because she's our…my," Kathy had corrected herself, remembering Pete was gone. "My little ray of sunshine.'

Sunny. She had been then. A happy, smiling child, her eyes bright, her golden curls dancing as she pranced around. Too young then to realize that her daddy was dead.

She was not too young now. She was keenly aware that her mother had suddenly disappeared from her life. He hadn't seen her smile once. But he felt a tug of admiration for the staunch little figure…bravely reassuring her brother while tightly clutching her own security…the bear.

His eyes burned, his heart aching for both of them, the boy who didn't understand, and the girl who did.

What right have I to complain, he thought, holding his sticky hands away from his clothes as the plane sped slowly down the runway, and gathered speed to take off. With the help of the Flight attendant they were all buckled in. He had placed both children in the window seat, and they were dreamily staring out, headed, he hoped, for sleep. When the plane was aloft, he could get washed up, open his newspaper…

Newspaper, hell! He had more on his hands than peppermint candy.

He had been right about Kathy Byrd. She had made careful plans, all documented in a living trust. But he couldn't quite grasp it when Mr. Canson, the lawyer, informed him that Kathy had named him guardian for the children and left everything she owned to him, in trust for the children.

"Me?" he had asked. "I'm not even a relative."

The lawyer reminded him that Kathy had no relatives.

"But she's never said anything to me. Surely there must be someone else."

"No," Canson assured him. "Only you."

Tray stared at him. The trust, the financial part, he could handle, supplementing funds if necessary. He would see that the children were never in want.

"But the children themselves," he said in some consternation. "I can't possibly take them. I'm a bachelor. No wife, no home even. I'm living in a hotel."

Mr. Canson could see his point. "Well, as guardian, your only responsibility is to see that they are given proper care." He cleared his throat. "Perhaps there's a relative who would be willing to—"

"No." Tray thought of his father, in his bachelor apartment. An aunt…on a cruise somewhere, he thought. This was crazy. A person couldn't will her children to someone, could she?

"I can see that this places you in a rather awkward position," the attorney said. "But I think we can arrange something. There is an agency available here for help in this kind of situation. I'll get in touch and arrange for a temporary placement.''

''That might be the thing to do.'' What had Kathy been thinking? ''She never mentioned anything about this to me,'' he said.

''Perhaps in the letter,'' Canson suggested, gesturing at the documents he had handed Tray.

''Oh.'' Tray had been so stunned, he hadn't even glanced at the papers. He opened the letter.

After reading it, no way could he place the children, even temporarily, with some agency.

He looked at them. Both asleep. The seat belt light was off. He went to the bathroom, washed his hands and dashed cold water over his face. He returned to his seat and took out the letter.

Dear Tray,

I hope you never read this letter. And maybe you won't. I'm only twenty-five and perfectly healthy. But Pete was only twenty-six when he left us all alone, and I'm scared. What would happen to Peter and Sunny if I weren't here?

If anything does happen to me, and I'm praying with all my heart it doesn't, then…this is why you have this letter.

Why you? Because you're the only person in all this world that I trust. And because yours was the only happy home I knew. Only a small part, it is true, but you cannot possibly know how much I cherished every minute spent at your house. All the laughter under that big oak tree or in the pool, even helping your mother make sandwiches or clean the kitchen. Do you remember how we made homemade ice cream in that old freezer, and everybody wanted the dasher? And always your mother smiling her warm smile. I used to pretend that it was my home, and I wouldn't be returning to the orphanage where I was one among many forgotten kids.

To be honest, the Home was the best place I ever lived. All the foster homes were horrible, and I don't even want to think about the Youth Authority. You didn't know I did time there, did you? Kids can get turned around. I don't want that to happen to my children.

Promise me, Tray, that it won't. I know you're not married yet, and might not want to keep them yourself. If not, please find someone...someone who really wants them and will love them, and give them the kind of home you had. Please, for God's sake, don't let them get caught in the system like I was. Please, Tray. Do this for me.

Again, I hope you never read this letter. But, just in case... Thank you for sharing your home with me, and thank you for finding that kind of home for Sunny and Peter. I love you,

Kathy

CHAPTER THREE

ON HER knees, Lisa mopped her way out of the second upstairs bathroom. She stood in the hall, rubbed an aching shoulder and looked back at the gleaming tiles covering the long counter, the clear mirror above, the spotless floor beneath. Stain-free. Sweet smelling. Perfect. Bleach along with that fragrant tile cleaner worked miracles.

And havoc on me, she thought, glancing at her red hands and broken nails. Rubber gloves slowed her down, and time was a precious commodity. Her chopped off hair was also a time-saver. Just wash and blow!

Money saver, too. No weekly trips to the beauty shop. Chic and smooth not required in this business, she thought as she picked up her pail.

Still, skimping on beauty treatments hardly made a dent in the monthly bills. I'm cleaning houses like crazy and getting further and further in debt. Harder work, less pay.

Talk about hard labor! Talk about time! On her first job, it had taken the whole day for her to do one house. But the real kicker had come when the lady of the house said she would not need her again.

She was still trying to recover from the shock when Joline showed up that evening with more referrals. No downsizing in the housecleaning industry. But qualifications were stiff, she thought, rubbing her aching muscles.

"I don't know if I'd better take those on," she said, burning with shame. "Mrs. Smith fired me,"

"She can't fire you," Joline said.

"Call it what you like. She made it clear that my services were no longer required."

"By her! That don't mean they ain't required by somebody else. Look, I got three places here. They want somebody bad."

Lisa wasn't listening. She was reliving the frustrating day. "I wouldn't want me back, either. I couldn't get the stains out of the bathtub and the windows still looked grimy."

"You gotta use bleach on stains. And—" Joline stopped, stared at Lisa. "Windows? You ain't 'sposed to do no windows."

"She said just the downstairs one, and—"

"She don't say! You say. What you gonna do and what you ain't."

"But if she's hiring me…"

"She ain't. You applying for the job."

"Oh. That's…different?"

Joline shook her head. "I can see you don't know nothing 'bout running no business."

"Well…" Not the time to mention her business degree.

"But don't worry. I'm gonna tell you how. You been real good to me, Lisa. You always gave me clothes for my daughter, and you paid me extra that time my boy got sick. Now you in a bind, and I'm gonna help you out."

Lisa was touched. "You've been good to me, too.

I really appreciate the referrals, but maybe I'm in over my head in this area." If cleaning houses was a business, she was clearly unprepared. Picking up her clothes before the cleaning lady came wasn't much experience.

"Shucks! Nothing to it. All you have to do is get straight what you gonna do 'fore you start."

"You mean make a contract?" Lisa chuckled. When the mind makes a contract the body can't fill... "You still have to do the job. I know that much."

"Oh, you can do it. You listen to me, and you listen good. No, you better write it down. Get a paper and pencil while I pour us some more coffee."

Writing is more in my line, Lisa thought as she picked up a pen. But she could hardly keep up as Joline rattled off a mind boggling list of do's and don'ts. "*Don't* do nothing by the hour. Charge by the job, and *do* check size of the house and how the folks live in it 'fore you set the price. Some folks live like pigs. *Do* list equipment and supplies needed. *Don't* supply none of these yourself. That way you ain't loaded down and you ain't bringing nothing in with you and you ain't taking nothing out. Some folks are funny 'bout what you taking out."

This is a business, and an extremely complicated one, Lisa thought as Joline listed supplies needed for special problems as well as a definite agenda. "Always do one floor at a time. That way you don't get plumb wore out, traipsing up and down all them stairs a million times. Hey, you ain't wore out yet, are you? We just talking about it."

"I know." But just <u>thinking</u> of the hard physical labor to which she was unaccustomed. "Today was...difficult," she said."

"Forget today. Nothing to it if you do it right. Tell you what...I'll go with you a couple of times and show you how to move along. Shucks! If you do houses in the same area on the same day of the week, you *don't* spend no time fighting traffic, and you can do two, maybe three houses a day."

So she was doing it! Two houses a day was keeping her employed, but it wasn't keeping up with expenses.

If she moved from her costly apartment...

Shucks, this was only temporary. When she got a real job...

But two short months seemed like ten years, and no sign of a real job yet.

She was worried.

Tray Kingsley was noted for his business sense. With keen perception, he took instant command of any situation, knowing instinctively who should do what. As easy as breathing, to raise his hand, point a finger...direct.

But when he entered the lobby of his San Francisco hotel with the girl, the boy and the teddy bear, he was at a complete loss. He hadn't a clue what was to be done nor who could do it.

"Mr. Kingsley, you're back! And with company. How nice!" The desk clerk's affability did not quite mask her surprise and curiosity. She leaned across the desk and smiled at Sunny. "Such a pretty little girl! What's your name?"

Sunny didn't answer. In total silence, she hugged her bear, held on to Tray's hand, her eyes seeming to grow bigger as she stared at the woman.

Tray couldn't speak, either, so unnerved was he by what he read in Sunny's eyes. More clearly than if she had spoken aloud, the eyes revealed what she was feeling. The absence of all that was familiar and dear. The strangeness of the new and unfamiliar…big…crowded. The loneliness…the terror.

He saw what she saw, felt what she felt. Too much weight for that staunch little shoulder. He wished—

"We are happy to have you and your little brother with us." The clerk smiled at Sunny, then turned to him. "We made the change you requested, Mr. Kingsley. Your things has been moved to the two-bedroom suite, 584."

"Thank you. I appreciate that," he said, about to release the girl's hand to take the key. But the tiny hand closed around his big finger and held on. He shifted the boy slightly, and accepted the key with his left hand. "Thank you," he said. "Now about the children. I spoke with a Mr. Dancy about arrangements for baby-sitting."

"Yes. I am sorry that our hotel program is limited to much older children. However, we do have a recommendation for you. Many of our patrons have used Nanny, Inc. from time to time, and found them reliable." She passed a card and a folder to him which he also took in the hand that held the boy. "If there is any other way we can be of service, please let us know."

"Thank you," he said again. He followed the

bellboy, his mind in a whirl. All hell was breaking loose at the office, which was normal and expected during this period of drastic change. He'd kept in touch by fax or phone almost every hour of the five days he'd been away, but it wasn't the same as being there. Especially when he was simultaneously trying to grapple with this unexpected turn of events in his personal life.

Well, too late to get to the office this afternoon. Should he try to meet with Sam tonight? He wanted to have everything in hand for the board meeting in New York on Wednesday.

It was essential that he be at the office in the morning. On a plane Tuesday, headed for New York. He had to see that the children were taken care of. He'd phone that Nanny place immediately.

In the elevator the bell boy tried to talk to Peter, but the boy only buried his face in Tray's chest, his arms a noose around his neck. The girl's hand stuck like glue. The message louder than words. *You are all we have to hold onto.*

He felt burdened. Responsible. Awkward.

"All right! We're here," he said, a bantering glad to be home ring in his voice. "Sunny, reach into my back pocket and see if you can find my wallet. That's a good girl! Thank you. Now, you hold on to Peter while I take care of this gentleman," he said, standing the boy beside her.

The door closed behind the bellboy, and Tray took a look at the stark and cold perfection of the hotel suite. He should have ordered flowers, fruit. No. Toys, books, or...something.

Her cry startled him. "I don't...don't like it

here!'' The broken sentences tumbled out between
a spasm of angry, helpless sobs. ''I want…want…to
go…I want to go…go home!''

She was still holding onto her brother and her
bear, but she was no longer the staunch protector.
Just a tiny lost and lonely child. The boy, following
her lead, added his cries to hers, and the tumult filled
the room, tearing him apart.

He bent to his knees, gathered them in his arms
and held them close. Their tears wet his face as their
bodies heaved against him in hot convulsive sobs
that broke his heart.

''That's right. Let it all out,'' he whispered. It was
too much. No way could they hold it in.

What to do!

''I miss your Mommy, too,'' he said, guided by
pure instinct. ''I knew her when she was a little girl
just like you.'' Not altogether true. Kathy had been
much older than Sunny when she first came to play
in his yard.

It worked. Sunny choked back a sob and her eyes
widened with interest. ''You did? You saw Mommy
when she was little like me?''''

He nodded, and her questions were eager and
rapid. ''Did she look like me…have a bear like
mine? Could she read?''

He sat on the floor, settling them against him, as
he talked about Kathy with colorful, exaggerated details that soon had them giggling. After that, it was
easier. They consumed some of the peanut butter
sandwiches and hot chocolate he'd ordered, splashed
in the tub for a short while, helped him find pajamas
and books in their luggage. The suite was a mess,

but he finally settled them together in one bed and read to them as instructed. "That's what Mommy does."

It was after ten when he picked up the phone in his own room. Thank God Nanny, Incorporated was a round-the-clock, twenty-four-hour operation.

"I'm a little worried about my grandfather," Lisa told Joline. "He's acting...well, not like himself."

"Oh? How?"

"Grandma said he got into an altercation with a man at lunch one day. Over passing the salt of all things," Lisa said, trying to picture her affable, always agreeable grandfather in an altercation with anybody about anything. "And Grandma says he gets very confused at the bridge table."

"That's too bad. Has he seen a doctor?"

"Yes. Grandma finally got him to go, and she talked to the doctor later."

"And?"

"He's not sure. Maybe just aging he says. Lots of people get irritable when they get older it seems. And forgetful. But Grandpa has always been so mild-mannered. I'm worried."

"Guess so. Do you think he could be getting that...what is it so many old people are getting now? Alls...something. Mrs. Salter, a lady I work for, says her father got so he didn't even know her."

"Oh, Joline, don't mention that for goodness' sake. I couldn't stand that."

"Couldn't pay for it neither I reckon. Them places is awful expensive, Mrs. Salter says."

"Oh, we wouldn't have to worry about that. My

grandparents bought into that senior complex which guarantees continuing life care without raising the cost. That's why gramps insisted it was the best place. He said he didn't want me to have that burden in case either of them became ill.''

''That's the best way. Be prepared.''

''Yes. Grandpa was like that. Extravagant, especially where I was concerned. But really smart.'' She chuckled. ''So why am I worried about something like Alzheimer's? Whatever happens, Gramps's not likely to lose that sharp mind of his.''

The phone rang, and she picked it up.

''Hello, Lisa,'' came the voice of Mrs. Dunn, whose house she cleaned every Thursday. ''I'm calling for a neighbor, a family that just moved in next door. They are desperately in need of a cleaning person, possibly twice a week. Interested?''

''I certainly am.'' Twice a week. She needed as many jobs as she could get. It was getting harder and harder to make the money for her grandparents and take care of herself too. If she didn't get a decent job soon—

''Good. It's the house on the right, 168 Pine Grove. This is the phone number... The name is Kingsley.''

Lisa wrote down the number and slowly replaced the phone, wondering...Kingsley. Why did that name ring a bell?

CHAPTER FOUR

THE Dunn's house, always a mess, had taken all morning. It was well after one when she rang the bell at 168 Pine Grove.

The door cracked open, and a small girl peered up at her, eyes wide. "It's not your turn," she announced.

"My...turn?"

"Bronsie's already here."

Had she come too late? The man said afternoon was quite all right. The man! Perhaps... "Could I please speak with your mother?"

"You can't. Tangled curls danced as the child shook her head. "Mommy's in heaven and she's never coming back. She—"

"Sunny! Who you talking to?" The shout from the back of the house was followed by the lumbering steps of a heavy woman wearing a light blue uniform. "I told you not to open the door."

"You said don't let anybody in. I didn't."

"Never mind that. Go up and see about your brother 'fore he gets into something."

Her eyes still on Lisa, the child backed away to obediently mount the stairs.

"And you keep quiet! Don't wake him up if he's still asleep. Which I hope to God he is," the woman said to Lisa. "He don't set still a minute. Come

43

on in,'' she added, opening the door to admit her. ''I reckon you the cleaning lady?''

''Yes. I'm Lisa, Lisa Reynolds.''

''I'm Mae Bronson, from Nanny, Incorporated, and I'm mighty glad to see you. This place is a wreck. Ain't no hotel. Might as well be camping out. Nobody picking up nothing, or—''

''Well, I'm here now. If you'll just show me—''

''Right. He said you'd be here and I was listening for you, but I sure didn't hear the bell. Lord, such a commotion! Angela telling Ken she's pregnant, and he—''

''Angela?'' Lisa gave a wary glance over the woman's shoulder.

''That's her name, but she ain't no Angel. She's a she devil if there ever was one. In that soap, *The Turning World.* You watch it?''

''No. I—''

''That bitch ain't no more pregnant than I am. But she knows he's in love with Kathy and she mean to put a stop to that! Lord, the messes people get into. You see… Huh? Oh, yeah, supplies. Back here.'' She led Lisa to a washroom at the back of the house.

''Thank you.'' It was all there: washer, dryer, vacuum cleaner and a pail full of cleaning rags and supplies she had requested. Except for the washer and dryer, everything, even the cleaning rags, brand-new. ''I'll start upstairs, if that's okay with you,'' she said.

''Just don't wake that boy. Oh, the mister left this for you.'' Mae reached into her pocket and handed Lisa an envelope. ''He say you're to clean everywhere, just don't touch his desk. In his bedroom.

Upstairs. You'll see it. And see what that girl is up to, will you? Can't leave those kids alone a hot minute. Gotta get back. Time for *County Hospital*.'' She darted off, leaving Lisa to find her own way.

It did look as if they were camping out, Lisa thought, as she wandered through the house. Probably the household furnishings from their former residence hadn't yet arrived. No dishes or cooking utensils, and all the downstairs rooms empty, except the sparsely furnished one where the nanny was seated before a blasting television.

And Mae Bronson was right about nobody picking up anything. Paper cartons and leftover food of the takeout variety littered the kitchen counter and built-in breakfast booth.

Upstairs, the first bedroom she looked into was a wreck...two rumpled twin beds, a chest, small clothes and toys covering the chest and toys scattered on the floor. But Lisa focused on the children, the small boy who, thumb in mouth, slept in one bed, and the girl who sat on the other, hugging a teddy bear. The girl sat so still and quiet, her blue eyes so lost and forlorn, that a lump rose in Lisa's throat.

She said the first thing that came to mind. "I'm so glad you're here."

The girl looked doubtful.

"I thought you might help me. Show me where to clean," she whispered. That was a silly thing to say. Everywhere needed cleaning. But if she could involve this child...

"Nannies don't clean."

"I'm not a nanny. I'm the cleaning lady."

"Oh."

Lisa spoke softly, as if in confidence. "Not in here because he's asleep. But you could show me which rooms are which and where to put things, so I wouldn't do anything wrong."

"All right." The girl placed the bear carefully on the bed and tiptoed from the room.

Lisa followed to a bathroom, which, as she had suspected, was right next to the children's room. And just as messy.

"These are Peter's." The child picked up a sock and shirt from the floor. "Tray said we should put dirty clothes in here, but Peter can't," she said, pulling open a built-in hamper.

The hamper was full. Evidently nannies didn't wash, either. "Peter's your little brother?"

"Yes. He's just three years old."

"And you're what? Six?" Lisa replaced the top on the tube of toothpaste, and began to clear the counter.

"Almost."

"And what's your name?"

"Sunny. Only it's really Chelsea, but everybody calls me Sunny."

"That's nice. My name is Lisa and that's what everybody calls me...plain old Lisa."

Sunny giggled. Lisa wished she could say something funny that would keep that giggle going.

"That's my toothbrush, the pink one and it goes in this cup. The other one is Peter's and that's his cup."

"Thank you. You're such a help. I want to get things right so your daddy will be pleased."

"Tray's not my daddy."

"Oh? He's your...?" What? Uncle? Grandpa?

"Just Tray. He knew my mommy."

"I see." *Knew* her? What did that mean?

"He was with us, but then he left. I was little like Peter and I don't remember."

"Oh." Abandoned her with two small children? The low-down dirty—

"But when mommy went to heaven she told him to take care of us."

Good for her! However she managed it. He ought to take care of his own children.

"So he came and got us, only we didn't want to go on account of we couldn't bring Spot."

"Who's Spot?"

"Our dog, but Tray said they don't allow dogs in the hotel where we stayed until we came here."

"I see." Hotel. That explains the lack of furniture. He'd been traveling light.

"And we couldn't bring Spot here 'cause this is tempo...tempo something. Tray says that means we won't be here long, but he said at least we could play in the yard only we can't." She hadn't brought back the giggle, but she had certainly loosened the child's tongue. "Can't play in the yard because Bronsie has to watch her stories, and Marylee, who comes most mornings has to study. Tray took us to the zoo and Peter was scared of the elephant. Tray works most all the time, even at night sometimes and a long way away like in New York and sometimes Cora had to stay nights and she likes scary movies. Do you like scary movies?"

"No, I don't!" Lisa gave her mopping rag a vicious twist, wishing it was somebody's neck! "Oh, sorry!" she muttered as she backed into something. She turned to see the boy huddle behind his sister. She smiled at him. "You can't hide from me. I see you. And I know who you are, too. You're Barney. Barney the dinosaur!"

He shook his head. Sunny giggled.

"You're not? Wait…I know. Of course. You're Arthur the aardvark, because he has a sister and you have a sister, too. You're not Arthur?"

"She's teasing," Sunny said. "I told her you're Peter."

"That's right. I forgot. Peter." Lisa set her pail on the counter and took the boy's hand. "Well, come along Mr. Peter, Peter, pumpkin eater. You can help me, too."

Both children followed as she went about her chores. She tried to keep them entertained as she worked, talking about children's programs remembered from her baby-sitting days, reciting Mother Goose rhymes her grandmother had quoted to her. And listened to them talk about Tray…what he did, what he said, what he liked.

The name kept bugging her. Tray. Tray Kingsley. Where had she heard it before?

She found out when she cleaned the master bedroom. Okay, she didn't touch the desk. But the wastebasket overflowed with business papers. Papers addressed to Mr. Tray Kingsley, Vice President, Lawson Enterprises.

Recognition dawned. It was he! The big shot who had sat on his backside in his New York office and fired her! Messed up her life. Just as he had messed up that woman's life. And, as far as she could see, was not doing right by their two children.

So Mr. Big Shot himself, had come to take over CTI, now Lawson Enterprises. And he would probably make a mess of that!

Rage churned within her as she stripped beds, washed and cleaned. She was hard put to keep up those silly rhymes that kept the children giggling.

She was finishing up downstairs when the caterer arrived with dinner. Nannies didn't cook, either. She wouldn't have accepted Mrs. Bronson's invitation to dine with them, except that the food smelled so good and she had skipped lunch. Besides she deserved it. Hadn't she been doing the nanny's job, too!

Not getting paid for it, either! Her mouth dropped open when Mae revealed how much the round-the-clock nannies were being paid. "Extra, you see, for here," she explained right in front of the kids. "Worth it, too. You see, we ain't set up for this. What we do is hotel sitting…where somebody cleans every day, and you order up what you like or take the kids down to the diner. Like I told you, here we might as well be camping out." She glanced around the table. "Don't you like that, Peter? Sunny?"

It's too hot," Sunny said, and Peter pushed his plate away.

"Lord, these children don't want nothing but sugar pops," Mae said as she stood and refilled two plastic bowls with cereal and milk. "Don't throw what's left away, Lisa."

"I may as well take it home with me."

Lisa packed the leftovers, wiped up after the meal and took out the garbage. At least the house would be spotless when she left it.

CHAPTER FIVE

THREE weeks later when she again mounted the steps at 168 Pine Grove, she was bone-tired. There was certainly more labor than money in this occupation!

And this was not her field. She was qualified for that job in Minnesota. She had received a letter from a co-worker who had transferred to a company there. She wrote that there was an opening just made for Lisa.

Lisa had sent her résumé, but she was still hoping for something near this area. Minnesota was so far away. She couldn't, as she did now, drive the eighty miles to Sacramento every Sunday to check on her grandparents.

Grandma was really concerned about Gramps. She said he was getting more confused.

He doesn't seem confused to me, Lisa thought. She had played a game of Scrabble with him the last time she visited, and he was, if anything, even more sharp than usual. Beat her all to pieces, putting in words she hadn't known were in the dictionary.

Still, she wanted to be near, to see for herself that they were all right, had the attention and everything they needed. And it was best, especially for Gramps, that they remain among the friends they had known so long. Grandma said he seemed to be all right among familiar people and if his routine wasn't changed.

Anyway, Gramps is just fine. Grandma always overreacts to anything.

One move she could make. She could get out of her expensive condo. She remembered that Pam, in her old office, had been looking for a roommate. She hadn't kept in touch with her former staff, maybe because of embarrassment over her comedown. But..oh, what the hell! Tonight she would check with Pam to see if the offer was still open.

Then there would be the matter of what to do with her furniture! She had really gone all out when she moved into the one-bedroom apartment with its spacious living/dining area, not only furniture, but all the appurtenances...pictures, whatnot. It hadn't been cheap. She'd never get what she paid for all those things. Could she afford to store everything, she wondered as she reached for the bell.

This time the door was opened by Mae Bronson. "Oh, it's you. Come on in. I better let him know you're here," she said, and mounted the stairs. When she returned she was followed by the children. Both ran to Lisa.

"I didn't know you were coming," Sunny said. "We 'sposed to go to the park, but if you want me to help you I could—"

"No, you can't," Mae said. "We going to the park. Take your brother's hand and go on." She let the children out and turned to Lisa with a significant glance toward the stairs. "He home today," she said. "Making me miss my soaps 'cause he say the kids need fresh air. Ought to be in his office, out of town or somewhere 'stead of here telling me how to run things. Oh, he say tell you to go ahead and clean. Just don't bother him. Leave his room be. See you."

Lisa watched her depart green with envy. She rubbed her aching shoulder and considered what Mae was paid for taking a stroll in the park. *Getting all that fresh air while I clean the house and somebody else cooks her dinner.*

I could live with that.

The thought clicked, switching on the idea, like a light in the center of her mind. The harder she worked, the brighter it grew.

Tray Kingsley had escaped from his office early that afternoon. In relative privacy, he could review the agenda for tomorrow's staff meeting.

No escaping Herbert Lawson of Lawson Enterprises. He tried to hide his irritation as he spoke into the phone. "Yes, sir. You have a point." *Damn! They'd been talking expansion. Now...move the whole operation to the Philippines? That was like making a U-turn in the middle of the freeway."* But...such a major move, sir. We should thoroughly consider the pros and cons before... Right...yes, of course I'll be there." He rang off, careful not to slam down the phone. *The man was greedy. Instant profit mad. No thought of the long run. If we make the move he's contemplating, we'll...* Now who the hell is that?

The knock sounded again. "Mr. Kingsley?"

The cleaning lady. "Skip this room!" *Didn't that nanny tell her what I said?*

"I'd like to speak with you, sir, if I may."

"Not now! I'm very—" He broke off. It was Lawson he wanted to choke, not this poor woman. "Come in."

Lisa almost jumped. The gruff voice didn't sound welcoming, reminding her, "Don't bother him!"

Maybe she shouldn't...

The heck she shouldn't! Behind that door was the man who had taken her well-paying job away from her! He owed her, damn it! And she was darn tired of scrubbing other people's toilets for peanuts.

While he was handing out buckets of money to people for playing in the park with a couple of kids. And the dumb cluck didn't seem to know that what he was paying for wasn't getting done!

Still, he must know that his household was in a mess. If she could convince him that—

"Well? What do you want?" The voice was louder and more impatient.

She braced herself, and walked in. "I'm sorry to disturb you, Mr. Kingsley. I just wanted to...I... you..." What she meant to say blanked out. "You are..." The man in the elevator. He had held her in his arms, made her feel warm, safe and cared for. He had been so confident, competent and reassuring that... She blinked, trying to reconcile that gentle caring man with the man who had abandoned his children. Who, with the stroke of a pen, had turned her life upside down! Who—

"Yes?" He stared at her, wondering at his surprise. Why did he think that anyone who twice a week turned this place into some kind of well-scrubbed order must be big and strong and...well, certainly not this frail slip of a girl…woman, that is. Evidently older and stronger than she looked.

It was as if he was looking straight through to the inside of her, discerning every thought, knowing… Oh, God! He remembers all that screaming and crying and carrying on like an idiot in the elevator. He surely wouldn't hire—

"What is it, Ms.…Ms.…?"

He doesn't know! Doesn't know I'm that idiot! Thank goodness. She straightened, tried to gather her wits. "Lisa Reynolds, sir. I…er…" She tried to recall her carefully rehearsed speech. "There's something I'd like to discuss with you."

"Concerning?"

"Your household."

"My household?" he repeated, looking puzzled.

"I'm not here on a regular basis, sir, but I couldn't help noticing. You've gone to some trouble to arrange for the maintenance of this house and the care of the children. I couldn't help but notice that—" She stopped. Best not to point out that he's making a botch of it.

He seemed to read her thought, and sprang to the defence. "It was a sudden and unexpected responsibility."

She recalled Sunny's words, "Mommy sent for him from heaven." The creep had not expected to be saddled with his own kids!

Not the kind of man she preferred to work for. But… More money? Less work?

She took on a professional tone. "I wondered that you haven't considered down sizing and consolidation."

"Pardon?"

As if he'd never heard the term. "A matter of combining services and cutting personnel." Cut me out of a job, didn't you! "You must have heard of the procedure."

"Of course. In business. But you were speaking of my household."

"And the various businesses involved."

"Eh?"

"Nanny, Incorporated, Carter's Catering and Reynold's Cleaning, to begin with."

He smiled. "I see what you mean."

The smile threw her off. So open, honest, and…beguiling the way his eyes twinkled. She switched her gaze and surveyed the disheveled room with slow deliberation. "Then you must see that combining these services under the direction of one person would make for a smoother running and more efficient operation."

Perhaps. But for the short time we'll be here—"

"You're not remaining here?" That explained the lack of furniture.

"Just until I find a suitable…until the children are permanently settled."

"Settled?" She felt a prickle of anxiety.

"Yes." She waited, but he did not elaborate…as if it was none of her business. But what did he mean? Was he going to dump Sunny and Peter? Where? They had already been torn from mother, home, dog, everything familiar.

He seemed to be wondering why she was still there. But when she did not move, he made another attempt to explain. "Not perfect, I grant you. But a temporary situation we must all tolerate until I can make satisfactory arrangements for them.''

The unfeeling bastard! She wanted to fly at him with her fists. Take the kids herself. Throw her arms around them and protect them. She spoke quickly. ''Temporary needn't be intolerable!'' She softened her tone. ''That is, I could... I'm available.''

''Available?''

''That's what I wanted to discuss with you. You're hiring more than a few people to manage a temporary situation. That seems...'' ''Financially unfeasible'' was on the tip of her tongue, but she didn't say it. He didn't seem to mind the cost.

''Lots of things need doing.'' Again that smile. ''More than I bargained for.'' He sighed, and for a moment she felt sorry for him.

''I could do everything.''

''Everything?''

''I could do the cooking, cleaning, everything. For less money.'' Only a little less. She meant to charge him a bundle herself.

''Perhaps. But I don't feel it would be fair, Ms. Ms.?''

''Reynolds. Lisa Reynolds.''

''Ms. Reynolds. It would not be fair to hire you for such a short period.''

''That doesn't matter. That's my problem.'' She spoke rapidly now, her mind on the children. If she could bring some order and love into their lives... ''I'd take good care of them. I really would. I—'' She stopped. The way he was looking at her, she must sound unstable. She had to speak calmly, present the problem from his viewpoint. ''Think how much it would save you just to eliminate those expensive eight-hour nannies.''

He seemed to be studying her, and spoke quietly, as if to soothe her. ''That, Ms. Reynolds, is the main issue. Quite unprepared for the care of children, I had to depend upon the experts. No offense to you,'' he said, not meeting her eyes, ''but I had to be sure they were always in safe hands. Nanny, Incorporated came highly recommended, their personnel carefully checked.''

Somebody should check on Nanny, Incorporated, she thought. Well, at least he was making sure the kids wouldn't be molested or mistreated. ''I can supply good references, Mr. Kingsley, assuring you the children would be safe with me.''

He shook his head. ''I'm afraid this situation is too much for one person. I'm often away for several days at a time, and—''

''Then a live in housekeeper is what you need.'' She couldn't believe she was saying that. Live with someone she didn't even want to work for?

''I'm afraid I'm unprepared for that, too. As I explained, this situation is temporary. I've only a short lease on this house, it's unfurnished, and—''

''Then the benefit would be mutual. I am in a rather temporary situation myself.''

''Pardon?''

''I need to move.''

''Oh?''

''I'm changing jobs,'' she said, abandoning her temporary stint at heavy housecleaning, come what may. ''Taking a position more in my line.''

''Which necessitates a move?''

"Yes." She hastened to give a rational explanation. "A bit of a gap between jobs. A couple of months before I'm to report for the position in...Minnesota." She crossed her fingers.

She could tell he didn't believe her. "I see. A position in Minnesota?"

"More in my line." At least this much was true. "But since I'm not to be there for a couple of months, I...well, I don't want to extend the lease on my apartment."

"I see," he said again, but he sounded doubtful.

"I'd be perfectly willing to help you out during the two months And...well, it would be convenient to me to close my lease and store my few possessions here temporarily." Get rid of the expensive apartment and storage cost in one fell swoop. Her mind boggled at the thought.

"I'm not sure this is a—"

"A penny saved is a penny earned! You realize that I'm offering you a package deal, cleaning, cooking and child care. Certainly less costly than what you're now paying for all three services."

His eyes sharpened, and she knew his business mind was calculating the cost.

She was calculating, too. If he paid her a half, or even a third of what he was now paying for all three services... "I am sure you would find it a more satisfactory arrangement. And certainly better for the children," she couldn't help adding.

That made him look...distrustful? "Those references, Ms. Reynolds?"

"You'll have them within the week."

"Then we'll talk again, and consider your proposal,'' he said. She could tell he was dismissing, rather than considering her application.

Ha! Just you wait, she thought. During her teen years in Sacramento, she had sat with the children of several prestigious people, including those of the present governor.

Two weeks later, after five days in New York, Tray Kingsley arrived at the San Francisco airport at 10:00 p.m.—1:00 a.m. in New York. But he couldn't blame his weariness on the time change, he thought as he collected his luggage and wound through the milling crowd to his car. He was just plain tired of talking.

And getting nowhere.

Was he wrong? Lawson had lured him into the firm, paid an exceptionally high price to gain his expertise at negotiating mergers without upsetting the federal watchdogs on unfair business practices...monopolization in particular.

Personally it had been a good move. His high salary was nothing, compared to the bonuses and stock options. He was on easy street if he never did another day's work in his life. In fact, he was well on his way to being what he had determined to be when he was twelve. He chuckled, thinking of the prophecy he made that day his dad said they couldn't afford the new speed bike he wanted. ''I will get it! And when I grow up I'm gonna be rich enough to buy anything I want!'' Within two months he had the bike, earned it by adding a few odd jobs to his paper route.

He was still earning his way, he thought, as he

made the turn onto the freeway leading to Pine Grove. In his year and a half with Lawson Enterprises, company holdings had doubled, and profits tripled, as reflected by company stock, which had split twice. Would go higher and probably split again if they made the move to the Philippines...as soon as the dust settled.

And that, he realized, was what was bugging him. The dust. San Francisco CTI would be blown off the map, and he would be flying back and forth, negotiating the overseas deal.

He was turning off the freeway now, and his mind switched from business to the children. Not that they had ever been out of his mind. And more than ever on this trip, his first trip out of town without the security of the well-recommended Nanny, Incorporated. Maybe he shouldn't have allowed the Reynolds' woman to talk him into this housekeeping deal. He had been a bit skeptical about her.

But a live-in housekeeper was a more cohesive arrangement, and her references, which he had double checked, were excellent. He had called twice from New York, and the kids sounded okay.

Still, the Reynolds' woman had only been there a week before he left, and he hadn't been around enough to see how things were going.

That was the real problem. He wasn't around much *period*. He had to get those kids permanently settled. And he didn't have a clue how to go about it. Which was why he had talked it over with Chase. They were pretty close, and she knew his situation better than anyone else.

That may have been a mistake.

Or bad timing. She had probably expected a more romantic evening on the one night he was free to take her out to dinner.

At least she hadn't expected to be confronted with a problem. And certainly not this kind of problem. Her eyes had turned stormy, her voice sharp, as she demanded, "Just who are these children?"

"Sunny...that is, Chelsea and Peter Byrd. She's almost six and he's—"

"I repeat...who are they?"

"I am trying to tell you. Their mother was Kathy Byrd. She died and... Oh, it's a long story. The bottom line is the children are entrusted to me."

"Yours?"

"What?"

"I presume they are yours."

"Mine? I've never even been married."

She gave a short laugh. "So?"

"What do you mean by that?"

"I mean you don't need a marriage license to be a father!"

"Damn it Chase, I—" He broke off, the rage receding. Other people, particularly the hotel personnel, had made the same assumption. He hadn't bothered to correct it. It wasn't their business, but mainly because of the children. Hard to explain in front of them. "They're not mine," he quietly explained to Chase.

She stared at him. "This is incredible! Nobody can leave their kids to somebody without... Surely she must have consulted you."

"Believe me, it was as much a surprise to me as it is to you. But what could I do?"

"Do? You should have left them in Columbus. There are agencies for this kind of case."

"No." He couldn't think of Sunny and Peter as a "case." "I just couldn't leave them with strangers."

"You're practically a stranger, aren't you!" She shook her head in exasperation. "She surely didn't expect you to take personal charge of them. You are not equipped for this responsibility."

"You're right about that. But I do want to see them happily placed with someone who is right for them. The thing is, I don't really know how to go about it."

"Why, you have to turn them over to an adoption agency immediately."

Well...maybe." He hesitated. "But I don't know. Kathy expressly wished me to—"

"And you're still thinking of that woman and what she wanted. Think about yourself. You have responsibilities of your own. You're still living in a hotel and—"

"No. One of our employees transferred and I was able to lease his house. It's better for the children and—"

"Better for the children! What about you? I told you I was coming out to help you get properly settled and you've just latched on to any old thing to take care of a couple of brats that are nothing to you! This infuriates me. How dare she saddle you with her children? The way you tell it, she wasn't even close to you."

"No, but—"

"She came from nothing herself. Wanted to will her children into a rich family who—"

"We weren't rich," he said. "And she didn't want to will her children to anybody. She wanted to give them...wanted them to have..." He floundered, thinking of Kathy, those eyes so like Sunny's fixed adoringly on his mother, offering to do this or that, anything to be a part of the love and the warmth of a family. "She just wanted the best for them," he finished.

"Ha! So that's why she left them to you? A bachelor. No wife or family or..." Her eyes focused on him. "Who's taking care of them now?"

He explained about the nannies. "But I hired a housekeeper just before I left," he added, and his mind went back to Lisa. She was young and looked more lively than those nannies, and maybe one person would give them a kind of stability.

Stability? He wondered about her own stability. All that talk about some vague position in the distant future.

"You know what you are, Tray Kingsley! You're a patsy!" Her voice triggered his attention, and he saw that Chase was looking at him in a strange way. "A house and a housekeeper for a couple of stray kids who have been dumped into your lap." She sighed. "Someone needs to look after you, and I'd better get to it. Let's see... I'll call Page Cutley. She's on the board of the San Francisco Children's Home and several other welfare organizations." She laid her hand over his. "Poor baby. You leave those kids to me. I'll see to them."

He had looked down at the hand covering his, and

wondered...why didn't he want that hand on Sunny and Peter?

He was turning into the driveway now, and he noticed a light in the living room. She was probably a TV addict like the others.

CHAPTER SIX

HE PARKED in the garage beside the same battered Chevrolet that had been there when he left. The same, he thought, grinning. At least he wasn't coming home to a nanny he had never seen before who would inform him that he was later than expected and she was to be paid extra for the overtime

Well, that was what he had liked about Nanny, Incorporated. He could rely on them. Responsibility for the children weighed on him, especially when he was out of the area for several days. Nanny guaranteed that the children would never be left alone, no matter what.

So? She was here. There was her car to prove it. He reminded himself that her character references were excellent. The kids were probably snug in their beds, he decided as he pulled his luggage from the trunk.

Still, he braced himself, never knowing what to expect...Sunny, running to him, chatting cheerfully or conscientiously reporting a calamity like a stopped-up toilet that Peter didn't mean to do and Nanny shouldn't talk to him that way and did you bring us some more wings like you promised? That was Sunny, always cheerfully in charge.

And Peter's arms tight around his leg, holding on to the one familiar person in this dark, unfamiliar world into which he had been flung. Peter was scared. Twice Tray had awakened in the early dawn to find Peter beside him, holding tight in just that way.

They were becoming too attached to him.

I'm not a God, Peter. And I haven't quite figured out the best way to make your world safe again.

I'm scared, too.

The house was quiet. No bombarding children, no blasting television. Maybe she was also asleep, and had left the lights on as a safety measure.

She was not asleep. She was going through the list, checking the firms she meant to contact, when she heard him drive into the garage. She quickly snatched up her papers. This was no concern of his. Even though it was his fault. She wouldn't be going through this if he hadn't snatched her juicy job out from under her!

She checked her resentment, and chuckled. He didn't know what he had done to her and, for some crazy reason, she didn't want him to know. She would revel in his surprise when she left his employ to assume the position of...well, some big responsible position for one of these companies. Lots of companies in the L.A. area, or somewhere within a five-hundred-mile radius of Sacramento. A reasonable distance from her grandparents.

Why hadn't she thought of zeroing in on these California companies before?

She had been so darn sure she would get a job in the city. Discouraged when she didn't. So many turndowns after getting fired put a big dent in the old ego even if it was attributed to the new cutting costs maneuver, called downsizing. All the big companies seemed to have caught the bug. Scary! And when you needed money right away, you didn't have much time to branch out.

Anyway, after a day's round of housecleaning, who could think straight?

Well, she was thinking now. Getting rid of money problems had cleared her mind. Free room and board, plus the big salary she was getting, even for two months, would put her financially ahead for four, maybe five months. Gave her time. It had taken only a couple of days to move herself in, settle the house and children into a comfortable routine. Keeping the house in order was a cinch, and the children were a joy.

Mainly she had more of that precious commodity...time. Time to rest and think.

Time to plan. This situation was temporary and she needed permanent. Time to remember Joline's "just 'cause she don't need your services don't mean somebody else don't need 'em."

She would find that somebody else, she thought, hurriedly stuffing papers into her case.

"Good evening."

The deep voice startled her. She had heard the car, but he had come in so suddenly and quietly that... "Mr. Kingsley. You're back. I...didn't expect you...tonight, that is. You...you surprised me." Stop babbling, she told herself as she snapped the case shut. But why was he staring at her like that?

Those wide dark eyes looking up at him. He had seen them before. He knew it.

Of course. She was the cleaning lady, the new nanny. She'd been here when he left. The same woman. Face freshly scrubbed, hair chopped as if she'd gone at it with a butcher knife.

But that look, those eyes. He had seen them before. Where?

"Is...is something wrong?"

"No." He switched his gaze from her to focus on the room. Also disconcerting. It had been empty when he left. "It's different."

"You said I could bring my things." She sounded defiant.

"Yes. Of course. But..." *Her* things? The luxurious three-piece sofa in that cozy conversational arrangement, the plush cushions. The Renoir over the fireplace. That large potted palm. Shaded lamps that cast a warm glow over the room. When she spoke of storing her few possessions, he had pictured old and dowdy. These, if he was any judge, were new and damn expensive!

"It's all right, isn't it? You said—"

"Certainly." He loosened his tie. What kind of patronizing egotist was he! Who was he to speculate on who had the taste for such elegance or, more to the point, the means to acquire it? Cleaning houses? For this house twice a week, she only received—

"Is something wrong, Mr. Kingsley?"

"No. I was just wondering..." About her, he realized, noting the case she was holding. It had a professional look. Hadn't she mentioned a "position more in her line"? It had sounded like a lie, but... No one knew better than he how many professionals had been abruptly displaced.

"I hope you don't mind."

"Pardon?" Immersed in his own thoughts, he hadn't been listening.

"That I...well, spread my things around. I didn't want to just stack them, like in storage."

But that was exactly what she had said: "store my few possessions." Now that he thought about it, she had sounded pretty desperate. Something about not extending her lease. Good Lord! Had she been evicted? Some people live just one paycheck from the streets and, judging by her fine furniture, she just might be one of them.

"I hope you don't mind, Mr. Kingsley. I thought... Well, it does make things more comfortable, don't you think? More...more homey."

Too homey, he thought. Like she had moved in for a long spell. Had he made it clear that this was a temporary situation? "Ms...." What the devil was her name? "Lisa. I must remind you that we'll probably be here for a very short time."

"I know. I wouldn't be available very long anyway. Didn't I explain that I expect to take another position very soon?"

"Yes." But it had sounded so lame and trumped-up he hadn't believed her. Now he hoped to God it was true. He'd hate to have to dump her and her finery into the street. He felt a rush of responsibility for...this stranger, those kids. His luggage, which he still held, was suddenly heavy. He set it down.

"You look tired, Mr. Kingsley."

"Yes. A bit...bushed." How the devil had his life gotten so complicated? The kids. And now this woman who was evidently homeless.

"Are you hungry?"

"Well..." Maybe that was why he felt weak. Hadn't touched a thing on the plane.

"The children and I had chicken. Let me fix you a sandwich."

"No. Don't bother to—"

"No bother. It'll only take a jiffy," she called over her shoulder as she hurried out.

Accommodating, he thought, following her. Probably trying to... He stopped short. The dining room was also furnished. Small buffet. Small table, too, only four chairs. But...pictures and all those doodads on the buffet! How many "possessions" had she brought? It looked as if she was settling in for the duration. No wonder she was trying to appease him.

Well, she needn't think she could appease him into housing her for the next millennium. And she needn't play the homeless, helpless female bit, either!

Helpless be damned! That little woman didn't have a helpless bone in her body. A five minute consultation was all it had taken to wheedle him into giving her a job and housing. And she was very comfortably settled within a matter of...what was it? A week? Two at the most. Plus a sizable salary that should keep her pretty well fixed for some time! He had thought he was a master at negotiation, but she outdid him ten to—

"Would you like me to bring it or would you rather—" She broke off when she almost bumped into him.

"I'm on my way," he said, rather gruffly, not

sure whether he was mad at her or himself. But in just two rooms she had created a look of... permanence? That bothered him.

No new furniture in the kitchen, but it was also a surprise. Spotless. Not the usual clutter of empty cartons and overflowing garbage. Couldn't say she wasn't working for her pay. And she was right about it being less than he had been paying for, as she put it, all three services.

And I wasn't getting this kind of service, he admitted as he sat in the breakfast booth and bit into the sandwich. Delicious. He was hungry.

"I thought coffee might keep you awake, so I made tea. Do you like it?"

He tasted the hot, strange smelling brew. "Not bad," he conceded.

"This is called Sweet Dreams, and is supposed to induce sleep. It always knocks me out, even when I'm upset." She sat across from him, and sipped from a matching china cup.

China! "Your dishes?" he asked.

"Yes. I put them in the cabinet. It's more—"

"Homey," he supplied, unable to suppress a spurt of irritation.

"Convenient," she snapped. "It's quite impossible to serve a decent meal with a few plastic bowls and cups. Impossible to cook it, too," she added, displaying a bit of irritation herself.

"Look, I told you in the first place that this was a temporary setup. You knew I was not equipped for housekeeping."

"Which is why I offered you a package deal in return for a package deal." Again, there was that flash of defiance in her eyes. "Yes, these are my dishes, my coffeepot, my cooking utensils, a few of the possessions, which you agreed to store, and which I certainly need if I am to deliver my part of the bargain...cooking, cleaning and child care. I thought we had agreed this was mutually beneficial, but if you are not satisfied with the arrangement—"

"Now wait! I didn't say I wasn't satisfied." He wondered why he felt the need to apologize. To explain. "I didn't think about...incidentals."

"Incidentals? I assure you, Mr. Kingsley, that what I have brought into this house are only the bare necessities."

"Oh? Plus pictures, plants and the Lord knows what else."

"Would you have me dump them in the street? You said that I could bring my things."

"Yes, I did. I'm sorry. It's all right," he said, feeling ashamed. This poor woman was in a bind and he was acting like a jerk. "I'm just so used to traveling light. Not much in my New York apartment and that's where I'm based. I don't plan to be here but a hot minute."

"But I thought..." She hesitated. "You're not remaining here?"

"Just until I dismantle this computer company we've taken over—CTI."

"Dismantle it? Why?"

He found himself explaining that, too, perhaps more to himself than to her. "That wasn't the plan originally. Usually, after a takeover, we just reorganize." He bit into his sandwich, took a sip of tea, thinking about it. "Now Lawson wants to relocate."

"The whole operation?"

"Yes. And I'm not sure—" He broke off. What the hell did she know or care about his business! "Sorry. This isn't pertinent. It's just that I've been so involved with an altercation at the firm that I haven't given much thought to the situation here." His gesture encompassed the kitchen.

She seemed thoughtful, and miles from the kitchen. "But San Francisco is the commercial center for the West Coast, especially if you're aiming for the Far East."

"Exactly," he said, surprised that she understood. "And, in this particular case," he added, thinking of Fraser, "there are people I'd like to keep who might be reluctant to make a move."

"Right. Easier to move companies than it is to move people, like checkers on a board!"

He stared at her. The accusatory note put him on the defense. "Profit is the name of the game, Lisa. And when you take an overall view," he said, thinking about the mergers he had negotiated, "you are immediately aware of the duplication of services by companies or personnel, the best course is to—"

"Downsize and consolidate!" she snapped.

"Isn't that exactly what you advised me to do when you applied for this position?"

"Any woman with half a brain could run a household, Mr. Kingsley. Big business is different, and downsizing can be detrimental. Key personnel can be lost *in* the shuffle. Often the best scientists and technicians in the field."

"Oh, I doubt that. Managers are usually aware of which technician is making the major contribution."

"Managers are people," she said. "Subject to petty likes and dislikes, which may weigh more heavily on which Tom, Dick, or Harry to let go than what's good for the company. Another thing," she said, pointing a finger at him. "Often what appears to be duplication may be stimulation."

"How so?"

"Intercourse between personnel, an exchange of ideas and comparisons that might result in a better product—" She broke off, as if suddenly aware that he was studying her.

"You sound quite knowledgeable," he said. "Perhaps you've had experience in business?"

"Not enough to count!" Abruptly she stood up. "More tea? Anything?"

"No, but thank you. This was delicious and just what I needed," he said, watching her clear the table. She had evaded his question. "Miss Reynolds, your references adhered strictly to your character and how good you are with children. I wondered about other—"

"Speaking of children!" She rushed across the room and collected several papers which had been stuck to the door of the fridge. "These are your welcome home from Sunny and Peter," she said, placing the childish drawings before him.

He hadn't even asked about the children! Had been so involved with her that he hadn't thought about them.

"They had such fun making these," she said. "They wanted to surprise you."

He was surprised, and strangely pleased. In all the weeks he had had them, this was the first indication that the children had been happily occupied while he was away. And, he reminded himself, he was usually away.

"Sunny's are mostly hearts and flowers," Lisa said. "And isn't that just like her?"

"It's Sunny all right." All love and sunshine, he thought, looking at the crudely sketched hearts and colorful flowers. "I'll take these to my room," he said, standing and gathering them up. "So they will know that I treasure them."

"Do that. Peter's masterpieces are a bit…shall we say surrealistic? But surely you can tell that's a dinosaur." She looked up at him. "Do you know that Peter sees you as his own personal dinosaur who will protect him from this dangerous unknown world he inhabits?"

"Yes." Interesting, he thought, that she knew it, too. The kids weren't just "charges" to her…as they had been to the other nannies. She saw them as individuals, each with a special need and a personality all their own.

Come to think of it, Ms. Reynolds is quite a personality herself. So manipulative with that pleasing servility that you forget who's in charge! The way she had negotiated this housekeeping deal. He chuckled. Lawson should hire her! A clever conversationalist too, and—

"What time would you like breakfast, Mr. Kingsley?"

Not as plain as she first appeared, either. Beautiful eyes. And that smile. Just a polite, questioning smile, but such radiance! Eyes sparkling, lips parted

and curving just so. Provocative. Enticing. He bent
forward to touch—

Good God! What was he thinking!

And what the devil had she said? "Pardon?"

"I asked about breakfast. What time and—"

"No. I mean you needn't bother for me," he said,
surprised that his voice was steady. "I leave early
and I'll get coffee on the way." He cleared his
throat. "Well, it's been a long day. Good night,
Miss Reynolds."

CHAPTER SEVEN

His abrupt departure gave her a start. He was mad at her?

Or at himself. For sitting with his housekeeper?

He didn't seem to be that kind of snob.

Anyway, nobody was more of a snob than Grandma, and she always shared a snack with Sissie, their weekly cleaning lady, when she was on her break. And I can't count the cups of coffee over which Joline and I talked about everything from her corns to my finding a job.

I miss Joline.

Darn it, I miss everybody! Sam, Pam and Mike, all the office gang. I miss Chris and all the movies, dining, dancing, or just fooling around together. Okay, so I wasn't ready for too much togetherness, and was a bit relieved when he transferred. Now I even missed his phone calls. He must have found another steady, while I...

That was it! I'm starving for somebody to talk to! Gramps always said I was too much of an extrovert.

But, heck, cleaning houses is a lonely occupation. None of that laughing, joking, talking over or exchanging ideas while you worked, like at the office. And no energy to seek company after work. Maybe she hadn't realized what she was missing until now. Then tonight...

He had looked lonely, too, when he set down his

suitcase as if he had the weight of the world on his shoulders. She had felt sorry for him. Well, okay, partly sorry and partly determined to please him. She meant to keep this easy setup until she got back into the main stream.

Anyway, no trouble to fix a sandwich and a cup of tea.

The thing was, she started talking and couldn't seem to stop. So companionable, sitting across from him in the breakfast booth. There was something about the way he lifted his right eyebrow in that puzzled inquisitive way, that slow hesitant smile, the alert, attentive set of his head, as if he was really listening. Some people were so set on getting their own point across that they never heard what you said. He wasn't like that. It had been fun going toe-to-toe with him on every issue. She bet she made him think twice about his stupid merging, downsizing maneuvers, which could sure use some correcting.

He listened to what she said about Sunny and Peter, too. She was glad he had. She didn't know why, but, for some reason, his neglected kids adored him. His name was a constant refrain...what Tray said or did or didn't say or do.

He didn't seem to care that much about them. She remembered that he'd talked of getting them "permanently settled" as if it would be a long way from him. That bothered her. That was why she had made such a big deal out of their drawings. She felt an imperative need to make him understand how much he meant to them. For a moment, she thought he did understand. And cared. She was talking about the drawings when...

What the dickens had happened! He had looked at her, his gaze so intent that it made her nervous.

Then, when she asked about breakfast, he snapped at her as if he was mad.

Well, not mad exactly. But he had turned so brusque and hurried out as if...

Good Lord! Did he think she was coming on to him!

She had talked too much. All chummy, running her mouth like a babbling brook.

With a man she didn't even like! How could she like a man who could abandon his woman and children? Was ready to abandon his children yet again!

He didn't seem like that kind of man.

Not her business. Her job was to keep his house and take care of his children.

And keep out of his way! She sure didn't want him getting the wrong impression.

Tray Kingsley walked down Fifth Avenue toward the restaurant where he was to meet the lawyer from Seattle. His eye was on the little boy in front of him. About Peter's age, and just as frisky, he thought, as the boy skirted dangerously close to the curb and the sea of rushing taxis. He was about to reach for him, but the woman was before him.

The boy tugged at her hand and wailed. "Let me go!"

"But I don't want to lose you," she quietly answered. "And I certainly will should you walk on the curb and lose your balance."

"I want lose...!" The boy paused. "What's my balance?"

The woman defined the term in a child's vernacular to the listening boy.

Tray smiled at her as he walked ahead. She reminded him of Lisa. Lisa could always defuse a tirade by talking common sense. "I can't hear you while you're crying, Peter. Now. Tell me. What's the problem?" Often, just as that woman had, she turned the tirade into a learning experience.

Not that there were many tirades. More laughter than crying. For the first time since he had them, the kids seemed really content. Always singing some song, or quoting a ditty Lisa had taught them.

And, he finally admitted, it was a good thing she had spread her things around the house, too. Made it seem more homelike. In fact, the whole atmosphere had changed. Even the smell of the place...cookies just baked or a succulent and tempting aroma from something on the stove.

Too tempting, he thought, grinning. Those simple meals she prepared for the children were a pleasant change from restaurant food, and he found himself often phoning her. "I'll be home for dinner today, Lisa."

Well, what the hell! He was paying for it, wasn't he? And why shouldn't he stay put instead of traveling so much! Like today. Easy to have the Seattle lawyer come to him, instead of the other way around.

And what if he did like coming home to 168 Pine Grove. It was quiet and... No, not quiet! But it had that same happy, serene quality that had graced his boyhood home. Boy. Restful. And God knows he needed the rest. And he liked seeing the children so content.

The children. His first priority should be to get them permanently settled. He knew that. He just wasn't sure how to go about it. Kathy's "please don't let them get caught in the system" had him stumped.

Were adoption agencies part of the so-called system? He wished he could ask her.

Not knowing what to do, he had done nothing. No time right now anyway. Lawson had him jumping, simultaneously taking over a plant in Houston and merging with an airplane manufacturing plant in Seattle. The Seattle venture was a biggy.

And a bit scary, he thought with a wry chuckle. All those planes on which he was a constant passenger were directed as much by computers as pilots. Made one think twice about getting rid of any well-trained computer technician, regardless of duplication.

He smiled, reminded of Lisa's comment that duplication allowed for exchange of ideas that might result in a better product.

Surprising how many things reminded him of Lisa. That was strange, for she seemed more a background than a person Always busy at some household chore or with the children, retiring or retreating to her room as soon as they were in bed. Never alone with him. There had not been a repeat of the kind of companionship they had briefly shared that night in the kitchen.

He was sorry. It had been fun chatting with her.

Surprising how much she seemed to know about the wheeling and dealing that went on in business. Even her terminology was not that of a cleaning lady. If he could talk further with her, delve into her background...

So he liked talking with her! What was wrong with that? She was witty, challenging...

And busy! Doing what had been done by several people, and doing it better.

Maybe he should suggest...

That was stupid. What employer would suggest to an uncomplaining housekeeper that she had too heavy a load! He sure didn't want her to get the wrong idea.

There ought to be some way. He'd think about it after the conference in New York this weekend.

That was another thing. Sunday was her day off and he wouldn't get back until Monday evening. He'd have to ask her to stay with the kids.

Where did she go every Sunday?

Sunny told him when he returned from New York. As he entered the house from the garage Monday evening, he was met by both children.

"We rode on a train," Sunny announced.

"It was big," Peter said.

Lisa called from the kitchen. "Mr. Kingsley just got here, Sunny. He's tired. Don't pester him."

"We're not." Sunny looked up at him. "Don't you want to hear about the train?"

"I certainly do." He was not about to cut off this tiny fountain of information. He handed Sunny his briefcase. "You can carry this up for me while you tell me all about it."

"We were going in the car, but Lisa said the train would be a ad...adventure 'cause we had never been on a train."

"We had popcorn and I had a window," Peter said as the children followed him upstairs.

"I had a window, too," Sunny said. "Only I was riding backward and it was like everything was passing me."

He chuckled. "Like the train was standing still, huh?"

"Yeh. Did you ever go backward on a train."

"I certainly did. I know exactly what you mean." He hung his suit bag in the closet, shed his coat and loosened his tie.

"And where did you go on this train?"

"To Grandma's house," Peter said.

"She's not our grandma," Sunny informed him. "She's Lisa's, but she said we could pretend. And we call him Gramps just like Lisa does."

"It's a big house," Peter said.

"That's because lots of people live there," Sunny explained. "Old people like Grandma, but she really lives upstairs and has her own kitchen and everything."

"We played cards with Gramps. I win."

Sunny giggled, shaking her head. "We just let him. He can't even read the numbers. I can."

So that's where she went every Sunday. To see her grandparents who lived in a retirement home. In separate, and seemingly rather plush quarters. Must be well padded. Or...was Lisa footing the bill?

On what she made cleaning houses? No way!

Grandparents. What about her parents?

And why the devil did it bug him! His concern was job performance, not her personal life.

"Tastes as good as it smells," he said as he sampled the simple meal of fresh green beans, meat loaf and mashed potatoes, so fluffy they melted in his mouth.

"Thank you," Lisa said, pleased. "I always..." She paused, about to say how much she had enjoyed helping Grandma, who was a great cook. "I like to cook," she said.

"It shows. This beats Carter's Catering all to..."

"Grandma makes good cookies," Sunny said. "She gave us some to eat on the train."

"That was nice of her," Tray said. He looked at Lisa. "So you took the kids for a ride on the train."

"Yes." She had known the children would talk about it, but so what! She hadn't wanted to miss her weekly visit. "You don't mind, do you?"

"Of course not. As Sunny says, it was a great adventure for them. I take it, you were visiting your grandparents?"

She nodded.

"Grandma's nice," Sunny said. "She let me wear her high heels and squirt on some perfume."

"Gramps showed me how to play cards and I win," Peter said.

"Had a good time, huh?" Tray said, but his eyes were on Lisa. "Sacramento's your home?"

She nodded.

"And you've always lived there?"

"Until I moved here," she said, not mentioning

the college years. "Watch it, Peter!" Too late. She got up quickly to mop up the spilled juice, glad of the distraction. Glad, too, that the children's continuing chatter prevented any further questions. Her personal life was not his business.

The cellular phone, always beside him, rang. He picked it up. "Kingsley... Oh, hi! Yes, got in a few minutes ago. Sorry, I was in a rush. You did?" He glanced at Sunny. Frowned. "Look, let me call you back. I... Oh?" He stood, pointed to the apple pie, and mouthed "later" to Lisa.

"I ate my dinner," Peter said.

"Me, too. Can I have ice cream on mine?"

Lisa nodded, a finger to her mouth, trying to shush them.

But Tray was walking out, still talking. "Listen, Chase, I don't want to rush on this."

Not business. A lady named Chase. Lisa's mouth twitched. Definitely upper crust and not to be put off!

Not that she gave a hoot who she was!

She cleaned the kitchen and took the children for an after-dinner romp in the park. After their baths, bed and bedtime story, she retired to her own room with a book. It was almost midnight when she fell asleep.

She was awakened by Peter's screams. "Don't! Go away!"

Another nightmare. She was out of bed in an instant, and running down the hall.

Straight into Tray! She would have fallen, had not his arms enfolded her. "It's Peter," she gasped.

"I know. I heard him. You okay?"

She nodded, but he still supported her as they both went in to Peter

For a moment it was all confusion. Sunny and her bear getting in the way as she tried to explain, "Something scared him and I can't wake him up."

Lisa, trying to reach past her, to cuddle Peter.

Tray, lifting Peter. "Hush, buddy. It's all right. Nothing's going to bother you."

Then all was quiet, except for Peter's muffled sobs. "He...he was gonna get me."

"No. That was just a bad dream." Tray's voice was calm, comforting. "Nothing's going to get my boy. I'll take him in with me," he said to Lisa. "Go back to bed."

He was so gentle with him, Lisa thought later, as she lay in bed, Sunny and her bear beside her. And he had said "my boy." Maybe he does care for them.

But her last thought as she fell asleep was of that brief moment in the hall, his arms around herself, so gentle and yet so strong...a safe and happy haven. She'd had that feeling once before—in an elevator.

Tray was also thinking of that moment in the hall. Soft feminine curves that seemed to melt into him, and the scent of freshly shampooed hair.

Peter stirred, and he looked down at him. His breathing was deep and regular. Tray loosened his grip, moved him a little away and pulled the cover around the sleeping boy.

Then he lay on his back, his arms behind his head, pondering. Lisa. Lisa Reynolds. Something about her... What was it that tickled his memory?

CHAPTER EIGHT

Lisa had not told her grandparents of her change of occupation.

Goodness, what was she thinking? It was not a change of occupation! Just a temporary fill-in until she was back at her *real* work. In the meantime, she was still managing to send their monthly check, so they had no cause to worry about her.

The small deception was easy. Their treks to San Francisco had always been infrequent, and almost nonexistent since Gramps gave up freeway driving, which he said made him nervous. She was diligent about her weekly visits to them, so they felt no urge to visit her in the city.

However, her change of residence posed a communication problem. She wanted them to always be able to get in touch with her, but should her phone be answered by a child or a man, curiosity would be aroused. And hard to explain. She solved this problem by telling her grandparents that, to cut expenses, she had had her apartment phone disconnected, and was only using her cell phone.

This arrangement worked very well, since she kept the cell phone constantly with her, and out of the children's reach. She was not concerned about her employer's curiosity. Her private life was no concern of his.

She also referred all business calls to her cell

phone, and was more excited than alarmed when it rang at five that morning. Early, even from back east. But it could be a job offer and maybe she should take it.

It was her grandmother, and her voice was unsteady. "Lisa, I'm so worried. James is missing. I woke up at five this morning and—"

"Gramps? Missing? How...what happened?" As she listened, her panic grew. But she could tell Grandma was all to pieces and she tried to keep her voice calm. "There must be some explanation. Perhaps he went..." Where at this hour? And without telling anyone?

"I'm scared, Lisa. Like I told you, he gets so confused...like he's not sure where he is, and I—"

"Oh, Grandma, he's not...he's just fine. Now you stop worrying. I'll be there. Just as soon as I can."

But she kept hearing the words. "Confused. Not like himself."

Kept seeing Gramps. Warm, loving, laughing. A clever, strong unfailing support as long as she could remember.

A deep dread was building inside her.

Tray heard the tap on his door. He glanced down at Peter. Still sleeping.

He put on his robe and opened the door. "Lisa! A short nightie swirling above long slender legs. Damn provocative!

"I...I have to go," she said.

His eyes lifted to her face, and the illicit, erotic urging switched to concern. "Go? Where?""

"Sacramento. Right away."

"Why?" He had never seen her like this. Out of control.

He managed to decipher the garbled, almost unintelligible explanation. Her grandfather. Took off early this morning or last night. Missing? He tried to reassure her. "Only a few hours at most," he told her. "He probably had some reason to—"

"You don't understand. I..." She looked down at herself. "Must dress. Wanted you to know I'm leaving. The children," she muttered as she ran back to her room.

Damn. He didn't understand. But he understood one thing. She was in no condition to drive anywhere.

Sacramento. Eighty miles. Could he make it back for his noon meeting?

In any case, he dared not let her take off...well, not drunk but clearly out of it. No telling what would happen.

He felt the weight of responsibility descending on him as he dressed. How the hell had he got into this mess. A cleaning lady he hadn't even known until... Three? Four weeks ago?

He caught her as she was about to descend the stairs. "I'm driving you," he said, taking a firm grip on her arm

"What?" She still had that dazed look.

"You're in no condition to drive."

"Oh, I can make it."

"Not if you take the wheel in the state you're in. You're upset, half-awake, and half-dressed," he said, looking down at her rumpled, partially buttoned blouse. "You might need to stay over," he said, seizing upon some excuse to delay until he could make arrangements for the children. "You should pack a few things. Be prepared in case."

"Oh, yes. I didn't think. I'd better," she said and hurried back upstairs. He went into the kitchen, made a call to Nanny, Incorporated, and took down the coffeepot.

Then he remembered. That tea she had given him that first night. Supposed to induce sleep. It didn't. She kept making calls to her grandmother, speaking reassuringly to her, but getting more anxious and agitated herself. When Mrs. Bronson from Nanny, Incorporated arrived and they were on their way, he took the phone from her. "I think these calls are upsetting to your grandmother," he said. "Anyway, we'll be there soon."

"Yes," she agreed, docile again. But still agitated. She kept muttering a garbled explanation, more, he thought, to herself rather than to him. And, he discerned, as if she took the blame. "I didn't pay much attention, you see. Grandma kept saying he wasn't like himself. But I thought he was. At least every time I saw him. We played Scrabble and he... Well, he won. Every time. Just like always. I thought... I didn't think. I didn't think. I should have done something. But I thought Grandma was exaggerating."

He put his hand on hers. "You might be exaggerating now. Your grandfather may have had a perfectly good reason for leaving, and you may be making much ado about nothing."

"Yes. You're right." She was quiet after that, and

fell asleep about an hour out of Sacramento. He had to wake her for directions when he turned off the freeway.

The guard at the tall iron gates of the complex greeted Lisa with easy familiarity. "Good morning, Ms. Reynolds. I knew you'd be here. But everything's fine. Your grandpa got in twenty minutes ago."

"Oh, good! Thank you for telling me, George. I was so worried." As they drove through the gate, she turned to Tray. "I'm relieved, but mad, too. Why didn't he leave a note so we wouldn't have been so upset! And you needn't have..." She smiled at him. "But thank you. It was kind of you to drive me."

"Kind to myself." His lip twitched. "Didn't want to be prosecuted if you smashed into something."

"Oh, for goodness' sake, that's only if you let an intoxicated person..." She stopped. "I was in a bit of a tizzy, wasn't I?"

"You were."

"Well, you see I thought... Oh, never mind. I overreacted, just like Grandma. There!" She pointed to an imposing building. "You can park in that lot. I'll just go up and..." She hesitated, then spoke decisively. "Come up and meet my folks. We'll see what ungodly errand took Gramps off so early this morning. Then I'll drive you back. Okay?"

"Sounds like a good idea. I can catch up on my sleep and get back in time for my meeting," he agreed as they walked through an impressive lobby. When the children had told him of their visit, he had pictured a modest old folks' home. Not the spacious grounds, well-appointed structures, elegant people milling around. The cleaning lady's folks must be in better straits than she. And apparently in good shape, he thought as she led him up a flight of stairs to the second floor. They had rushed here for nothing.

He wasn't so sure when they reached the apartment. The three elderly women in the little sitting room seemed distressed. The small gray-haired woman flung herself into Lisa's arms. "Oh, Lisa, I'm so glad you're here!"

He saw the apprehension in Lisa's eyes, and was surprised by the steadiness of her voice. "Hush, now, It's all over."

"No, it's not! When they brought him back—"

"Brought him?" Lisa was as shocked as he. The man at the gate had inferred that he had driven in himself.

"Oh, Lisa!" It was a heartbroken wail and anxious words followed in rapid succession. "They've taken him...put him away somewhere. They say for security. Like he's not safe here and they're responsible. Lisa, you have to do something!"

He saw the stricken look on Lisa's face. With two women on his hands, how could he...?

But... He watched Lisa recover and speak confidently to her grandmother. "Now, now. It can't be as bad as you think. I'll call Mr. McDougal and... Wait. We're forgetting our manners. Grandma, this is Mr. Kingsley...my employer. And this is Mrs. Wilcox, my grandmother."

Lisa's words seemed to recall the woman to her

duties, and she turned to him. "Mr. Kingsley, I am sorry to have called Lisa from the office, but we, er, had a bit of an emergency. Oh, and my neighbors…"

He responded politely, but didn't even catch the names of the two women who soon went quietly away, saying, "Now that your daughter is here."

His mind wrestled with the realization that the situation was worse than they had supposed, and how the hell had he got into it. And what did she mean—called Lisa from the *office?*

Instinctively, however, his caring nature registered concern, and a feeling that he must do something. But what?

"Try to get her to take a little of this." Lisa handed him a small glass of brandy, and nodded toward her grandmother. "I have to make a call."

He coaxed the older woman to take a few sips while Lisa spoke quietly into the phone. He sat on the sofa beside her and was trying to think how to comfort her when Lisa put down the phone.

"Grandma," she said. "The main thing is that Gramps has returned safely. Now, we are going over to see him and he certainly won't like to see you upset. Go and wash your face and put on some lipstick. Go on now." Her grandmother went out and she turned to Tray. "I'm sorry, Mr. Kingsley. I need to see exactly how…how things are. I may have to stay. I'm not sure how long."

The way the firm set of her chin battled with the worry in her eyes pulled at him. "It may not be as bad as you think," he said. "I'll wait while you check."

"But you've been to so much trouble already."

"And am already here. A while longer wouldn't make much difference"

"Oh. Well, it shouldn't take long. If you don't mind…"

"Of course I don't mind. Take as long as you need." He couldn't just dump her and leave, could he? He decided he'd better call Sam and alert him to sit in on the meeting for him.

She smiled at her returning grandmother. "Now that's more like it. Let me fix your hair and we'll go down. I want to arrange for Mr. Kingsley to have breakfast. They're still serving and the food is good," she told him as they walked down the stairs. He had noticed there was an elevator, and wondered, thinking of Mrs. Wilcox, why they didn't use it.

The food was delicious and elegantly served. He was still sitting, enjoying a chat with two men at his table when she returned.

"I do appreciate your waiting, and I will be able to leave with you," she said. "I just have to fill out some papers, get my grandmother settled and I'll be with you shortly."

He watched her walk out, head erect, back straight, smiling and greeting other diners. The epitome of calm, cheerful efficiency.

He had thought…

Well, he was wrong. She needed him like she needed a hole in the head.

They were clearing things away when she came back, but she said she wasn't one bit hungry. "We'll get back in time for your meeting," she said as she walked briskly to the parking lot. She took the wheel

as promised and waved a cheerful goodbye to
George as she drove out of the gate. Apparently the
situation wasn't as crucial as it had appeared.
Anyway, apparently settled to her satisfaction. He
sat back, relieved.

Two blocks from the complex, she pulled to a
curb and stopped.

He sat up. What's wrong?''

''N…nothing. I just need to…to…'' Her voice
trailed off. Her hands were tight on the wheel, and
she seemed to be straining to catch her breath.

He reached over, switched off the engine and took
the key. He got out of the car, walked around to her
side and opened the door.

''I'm all right,'' she panted. ''I can drive.''

''Sure. But first, we'd better take a breather.'' He
did intend to drive, but when he saw a nearby coffee
shop, decided she needed food. Something.

Her turnabouts were unnerving. So spaced out this
morning he hadn't dared let her out on her own. A
moment ago she had been confident, self-contained.

Now… Hell and damnation! She was clearly fall-
ing apart!

A bowl of hot soup was all he could think to order
once he settled her in a booth in the diner. ''It's
been a long day. You'll feel better if you eat something.''

''Yes,'' she said, and made a valiant effort. But
the spoon dropped from her shaking fingers and, as
if she couldn't help it, she let go. Silently, head
erect, but as if she couldn't stop the tears raining
down her face.

Like Sunny. That first day in the hotel… ''I don't

like it here!'' After she had been so staunch, so protective of her little brother.

Just as Lisa had been staunch and protective of her grandparents. Hiding her own despair. *Until out of their sight.*

Now she had to let go.

He rounded the table, sat beside her and, as he had done for Sunny, cradled Lisa in his arms. ''There, there'' was all he could think to say.

She leaned against him, mopping her face. Her words tumbled out. ''Gramps. Oh, God, I couldn't believe it. He's like a little boy. No... Back to... This morning. He thought... He got up, dressed as he used to, Suit and tie... You see, he thought he had a meeting. The school was locked and...'' From her broken sentences he learned that her grandfather had Alzheimer's.

Her distress was acerbated by the conviction that she should have recognized and prevented it. ''Grandma kept telling me, you see. But I didn't believe it. I should have...''

''Hush!'' he said ''There's nothing you could have done.''

''Oh, yes. You see, Gramps and I were always close and I think if I—''

''Stop it!'' He shook her a little. ''You sound like me.''

''You?''

''When my mother died. We were close, too. I got it into my head that her massive heart attack was all my fault.'' He had her attention. She was quieter now and he kept talking. ''She didn't even want me to go away to school And then when my work took me farther away and I was so seldom home..." It had taken him a long time to come to grips with his own grief and guilt. Somehow it was a relief to share the feeling. "We don't like it when something bad happens to someone we love, but we can't shoulder the blame," he said. "Life's not perfect."

"I know you're right. It's just...seeing Gramps like that. Knowing I can't help him" She lifted her face to him. "It's...scary!"

He stared, transfixed. Jolted by a memory.

That head against his shoulder, terror in those wide eyes.

Once before...

In an elevator!

CHAPTER NINE

How had he missed it?

Easily. A different woman. Chic, professional. Got off on that floor and walked into an office as if she belonged there. He had thought—

She stirred, murmuring. He bent to catch the words. "Always there for me and now I can't be there for him."

"But you are."

"What?"

"This morning. You did what had to be done."

"But it tore me to pieces. And this is only the beginning. The doctor said he won't get better, but worse." Her eyes filled again. "And...oh, look at me now!"

"You deserve a good cry. Let it all out."

Afterward, she remembered. He understood. All the anger, guilt and fear exploding within her.

He had just held her.

When she grew quiet, he said her soup was cold, and placed another order.

It gave her the strength she needed. The hot soup, his sustaining arms, maybe what he said. Whatever. She managed to pull herself together, and...well, he didn't let her drive, but she was quite composed during the rest of the trip. At least she didn't go bonkers again!

Then when they got back, she didn't have the

chance. Peter and Sunny flew at her, almost knocking her down. "Lisa! You're back!" Both were bawling like crazy. She gathered that they thought she had gone forever.

While she tried to reassure them, Tray paid Mrs. Bronson and hurried out. "Must get to the office," he explained over the tumult. "I've already missed one meeting."

The door closed behind him, and Mae Bronson looked at Lisa. "He got you on full-time, huh? Pretty soft going. 'Cept them two kids done got plumb out of hand. All that yelling and carrying on. I couldn't hardly hear nothing on the telly. Still real picky, too. Didn't touch none of that pizza I ordered for their lunch. Big Boy Special, fifteen dollars. Oh, yeah, I forgot that! You got that much on hand? Thanks, he'll pay you back. I'll be outa here right after *This Turning World*. It's just coming on," she said, seating herself before the television. "Oh, don't throw that pizza out. They ain't gonna eat it. Might as well take it with me."

The world keeps turning, Lisa thought. She'd better move with it if she didn't want to fall off. She entertained the kids with a funny story while she cleaned the kitchen. How did so much mess accumulate in just one morning?

As the days passed, keeping a house in order and two children busy and happy kept her from dwelling on a problem she could do nothing about. The doctor at the complex had been right when he urged Lisa and her grandmother to return immediately to their usual routine. Better for both of them.

Grandma, with the bridge and planned outings with supportive friends seemed to be adjusting.

Better for Gramps, too, safe under a supervised routine. Grandma could visit him anytime she liked and Lisa now went twice weekly, taking the children with her when Tray was unavailable. Lisa saw that Grandma really enjoyed the children while she was with Gramps. Sometimes he didn't know her and sometimes he was his old self, even besting her in a game. Either way, he seemed happy. She had to be content with that.

Meanwhile, she reminded herself not to be too complacent. Mr. Kingsley had been much nicer than she had thought, had instructed her to take as much time as needed with her grandparents, frequently sending small gifts himself: books, flowers, candy. But this situation was temporary. She had to make a move, find a real job. And soon. She hoped not too far from Sacramento.

Tray realized the strain she was under and refrained from questioning her. At first.

But he could not restrain his curiosity.

Cleaning houses? It didn't add up. Her grandfather had been a well-respected educator, and she...

That day in the elevator...decidedly the same woman. And definitely a professional. She had the garb and the stance, and she had walked down that hall as if part of the organization. And, come to think about it, even in her conversation.

What the hell had happened? He could restrain himself no longer. He had to know.

"Lisa, could I ask you something?"

"Sure." She didn't look up from the pot she was scouring.

"What did you do before this?"

"Do?" Her hand tightened on the pot. For a long moment there was silence, broken only by the sound of the television and the giggles of the children in the den. Then she turned on the faucet, and spoke above the rush of rinse water. "What do you mean...do?"

"What kind of work?"

"I cleaned houses. You knew that. I worked for Mrs. Dunn next door, and she—"

"I mean before that."

She dried the pot, placed it on the counter and turned to face him. "Why?"

"I'm curious. I think...I know I've seen you before."

"Oh?"

"In an elevator. You got off at Computer Tech, and you weren't there to clean the office. Not in those high heels and that suit. And I believe you were carrying that same leather briefcase I've seen you with here."

"And you don't beat around the bush, do you? Okay. I worked there."

"I thought so. But...how is it I never saw you there after that day?"

"Because that was my last day with CTI,"

"I see," he said, wondering about that momentary flash of contempt in her eyes. Some altercation there? She had once said something about taking another position more in her line. "You decided to make a change?"

"No. I was fired. Thanks to a New York big shot with corporate takeover as his mission."

The contempt was aimed at him. But why? "So?" he questioned.

She looked straight at him. "His eye was on nothing but the market—stock market!"

"Always a consideration in mergers. Profit is the name of the game."

"Oh, sure." Her hand cut through the air. "Cut the overhead and up the profit!"

"Oh!" He was getting the picture. Mergers always meant staff changes. "Let's be specific. What's that got to do with you?"

"Middle management is the first to go!

"So that was your status. What area?"

"Research and development."

He felt a surge of admiration.

"CTI's most important aspect and the reason we wanted the merger."

"And you got what you wanted. Lawson Enterprises has that reputation."

"Get off our back. We didn't fire you."

"Reduced in force is the correct terminology. And if you didn't do it directly, you—"

"Okay, okay! You got a raw deal. New technology...a shift in the economy, and—" He stopped, as if to study her.

"Your experience and qualifications must be useful and more than adequate. I don't understand why the hell you had to resort to cleaning houses."

"Other companies had also caught the down sizing bug. At least in this area," she added.

"And you wanted to remain here?"

She nodded.

"Your grandparents."

She nodded again.

He was trying to figure it out. "You probably didn't rate a golden handshake, but there's usually some kind of bonus for—"

"After a year and a day?"

"Oh. Well, unemployment…"

"Puny, temporary and forever in a bureaucratic process. Have you ever been in one of those lines? And if you're in need of ready cash…"

His brow lifted.

She glared at him. "All right! I'm a spendthrift!"

His lips twitched. "I know."

"You don't know a darn thing about me!"

"I know you've done a remarkable job of furnishing, even decorating, this whole house with what you bought for a small one-bedroom apartment."

"It was a *large* apartment."

"From which you were about to be evicted."

"I was not! I still had the last month advance—"

"So you kept up with the rent…which couldn't have been cheap. Along with furniture and car notes I presume. And…" He thought of her efficient control at the senior complex, signing papers, her breakdown on the way back. "Your grandparents. Where they're living looks pretty plush. Are you paying for that, too?"

"Of course not! I only…" She took a deep breath. "My expenses are none of your business."

"No, of course not. But you must have been

cleaning houses like crazy until..." He chuckled. "You cleverly negotiated to dump the load on me."

"Dumped on you! You're making out like a fat rat in a cheese factory. And, I hasten to add, at less cost! You've no right to complain."

"I'm not! I'm not!" he said, almost choking with laughter. "Mutually beneficial just as you said. Oh, come now. Don't be angry with me. I'm in your corner. I admire your practicality and ingenuity. You did what you had to do, and you're doing it cheerfully. Having you here is like a breath of fresh air. Come over here and sit down," he said, leading her to the breakfast booth. "Let's talk."

She sat, feeling a little dizzy. He wasn't putting her down. Complimenting her?

"You're quite a woman, Lisa. You deserve more than...than this," he said, his gesture taking in the kitchen. "I'll get more coffee and we'll decide where we go from here."

"We?" She blinked. "I don't know about you, but I am very well prepared to take care of myself."

"You've proved that." He placed a cup of coffee before her, sat across from her and sipped from his own cup. "Nothing wrong with making plans. We both know this is temporary. And...well, you're qualified for a more lucrative and challenging position. I might be able to make an offer."

"No, thank you. Not at CTI, which you plan to dismantle!"

"And which necessitates a daily elevator trip to the forty-third floor," he added, chuckling.

She felt her cheeks grow hot. "Don't remind me. I did act like an idiot, didn't I?"

"Not like a gal who can swing with the punches, which you have proved you can do, Lisa." Again she saw a gleam of admiration in his eyes. "You must not have been accustomed to this kind of labor. And yet…well, you make it look easy."

"You think so? Ha! You should have seen me on that first day." She thought about it, and couldn't help laughing. "Honestly, if it hadn't been for Joline…"

He joined in her laughter as she told how Joline shared cleaning techniques and gave her excellent advice. "She ain't hiring, you applying… She don't say. You say what you gonna do and what you ain't… I can see you don't know nothing 'bout business, but I'm gonna learn you."

It was fun, reliving the experience with someone else. Joking about it. Appreciating Joline's keen philosophy. They had such a good time they forgot about the children. When they did remember, they found both Sunny and Peter fast asleep on the floor while an old movie droned on the television screen.

Lisa awoke the next morning feeling rejuvenated. The sun seemed brighter, the air fresher and she felt lighter on her feet as she danced in to rouse the children, "Get up, get up, you sleepyheads. It's time, it's time. Get out of bed."

Sunny ran to her, arms outstretched. "I like that song, Lisa. Did you make it up?"

"I guess I did." Didn't even know I was singing, she thought, as she hugged Sunny and reached over to tickle Peter.

"I like when you sing," Sunny said. "It makes me feel good."

"Me, too," Peter said, though convulsed in giggles.

"I feel pretty good myself," Lisa said. After last night. She was out of hiding, and could relax and be herself.

No, it wasn't just that. What was making her feel so good was the way he had reacted, what he said. Like mopping floors wasn't a come down, but a practical, ingenious thing to do. She flushed with pleasure as she remembered. "You're quite a woman, Lisa!"

And that was after she had put *him* down! Her face burned with shame as she recalled her snide jibes leveled at the New York big shot. Good Lord! His expertise was mergers. His prospectus of CTI had been routine; based on the usual better business procedure. And, as he had pointed out, nothing to do with her job. She shouldn't have been so critical and nasty. She winced.

Still…he hadn't minded, in fact had hardly noticed. He seemed more interested in her. In that calm, direct way of his, he had drawn it all out…what had happened and what she had done. As if he understood. She had even felt comfortable confiding in him, telling him about her blunders, and about Joline. What had seemed a nightmare when she was going through it had become an amusing adventure, something to joke about. She liked telling him, making him laugh. She liked the way he laughed…deep-throated, hearty, all-out. And his eyes would crinkle in that special—

"Lisa! I can't get Peter's shoe on!"

Good heavens! She had spaced out. Unaware of where she was…what she was doing! "That's the wrong shoe, Sunny. That's for the right foot. Try this one. You're such a sweet girl, helping your brother." While I sit here like a zombie. Dreaming about your dad, for Pete's sake. "Thank you, Sunny. Let's see. Your T-shirt is on backward. Now, get the brush and let me do your hair." She had to get herself together and her mind off that man.

It was hard to keep her mind off him since he was there even more than usual. There were fewer trips out of town, and dinner with them had become so routine—he even phoned when he would *not* be there.

Having him around was good for the children. She could tell they were forming a closer relationship. He played games with them, often took over the bedtime story and had a kind way of disciplining them. Or maybe it was that they took kindly to whatever he said. As far as the kids were concerned, Tray could do no wrong.

And, yes, he did care for them. He even made extra time for them. They had a couple of picnic dinners at the park, went to the circus, and when she took Sunny to the dentist, he had met them there. "Sunny was a little nervous, so I promised I'd be with her," he said, "and that we'd all go to Happy Burger's for lunch afterward." He was a good and understanding father. Surely he would keep them with him.

He had left them and their mother!

Well, there must have been some good reason. He wasn't a deserting kind of guy.

She shouldn't judge, especially a situation about which she knew nothing!

Whatever the situation, the children should not be detached from him again. He was a bachelor, and it wouldn't be easy. But if he found a good house-keeper...

Not her business. She'd better get herself attached to another job, before she was detached from this one. She was working at it, even had a couple of interviews scheduled in L.A.

Now why did that thought depress her?

She knew why, but she hated to admit it. She was becoming too attached to...to this temporary job. To the children, and like the children, to...

No! Surely not to the man himself! Not to those simple little excursions and games when he joined her and the children. Not the time spent with him after the children were in bed...the challenging debates, jokes and laughter, and those stupid hard-fought games of gin rummy.

And why the dickens did she never stop thinking about him...what he said, or the way he laughs, even that silly smirk on his face when he yells a triumphant "Gin!"

Yep! Time to go.

And one of the L.A. jobs did look promising.

CHAPTER TEN

"COMING with us, Tray?" Sam Fraser called as he started out to lunch.

"Nope. I think we've got things pretty well covered here. And I've got some pressing data at home I'd like to go over." Not exactly true, he thought as he pressed the elevator button for the parking garage. There was some data on his bedroom desk, but none of it was pressing.

So why was he heading home in the middle of a business day?

Because they really were up on things at the office, he had no appointments and could relax for this half day. The best place to relax was home.

Home? He gave a little chuckle. He had lived in dormitories, frat houses and over a dozen apartments, hotels and condos since he left for college fifteen years ago. Never had he thought of any one of them as *home.*

But there was something about the temporary rental on Pine Grove. Maybe because it was a house. Or maybe because of the children. Once or twice he had found neighborhood children playing in the yard or splashing in the pool, even the teenage Dunn boys from next door. Lisa said they helped look out for the little ones.

Lisa. It was Lisa who had changed the place into a home for Sunny and Peter.

It sure hadn't been like that with the catering service and all those nannies.

It was Lisa who had changed a cold and barren house into a bright haven, alive with fun and laughter and tempting smells from the oven. Where you felt warm, welcome and happy. The home his mother had created, and he had enjoyed all through his growing up years.

He had taken it for granted then. Hadn't even known he'd missed it. Until now.

But Kathy hadn't taken it for granted. She knew what she had been denied.

For the first time he really understood what Kathy asked of him. "A home like you had for Sunny and Peter."

She had said something else. "You're the one person in all the world that I trust."

He felt a stab of guilt. They were happy now, but this was temporary.

Not that he had been lagging in the search for a permanent home for them. Chase, more qualified than he in this sort of thing, was making inquiries. She had phoned yesterday to say she had some good leads, and would be in touch soon.

As he turned into the driveway, he thought of Lisa and felt another stab of guilt. He had contacts. Close contacts with key officials in several companies in the area. One word from him and she would be immediately placed in a position for which she was well qualified.

He was sure lagging on that. For purely selfish reasons. He needed her here. She made it so comfortable, even pleasant. And while he was responsible for the kids...

Well, he wouldn't leave her in the lurch! As soon as Peter and Sunny were happily settled, she would be placed in a permanent and very lucrative position in this area. He would see to that.

Naptime, he decided as he entered an unusually quiet house. Was Lisa napping, too?

She wasn't. She was on her knees scrubbing the kitchen floor.

"Get up from there!" Before he realized what he was doing, he had yanked her up, almost knocking over the pail.

"What...what's the matter?"

Damn if he knew. But something about her in those old cutoffs, on her bare knees, a mop rag in her hand, irritated the hell out of him. "You don't have to do that." His mother never had. She left such chores to him, or his dad, or to hired help the few times they could afford it.

She seemed puzzled. "The...the floor gets pretty sticky."

"But you..." He felt her wince and loosened his grip. But he couldn't release her. Couldn't move. Those wide blue eyes, so innocently seductive, the curve of that kissable mouth...

He took a deep breath. "You've got enough on your hands, Lisa. I'll tackle the floor. Just give me a minute to change." Unable to stop himself, he touched his lips to her forehead. "Can't have you working too hard," he muttered before he hurried away.

*   *   *

Joline bit into her sandwich, swallowed, and looked around the kitchen. "Pretty neat setup."

"Yes," Lisa said. "It is a nice house, isn't it?"

"Ain't talking 'bout the house. I'm talking 'bout the cozy do."

"Cozy?"

"Oh, come on, Lisa!" Joline lifted her cup. "Your dishes. Matter of fact, all your things…sofa, pictures, all them little doodads scattered everywhere. Like you right at home. Just wondering how you worked it!"

"I told you, er, that is, Mr. Kingsley had all these people coming in and I suggested—" She stopped. "But you know that. You helped me unload all my other cleaning jobs so I could take this job. I do appreciate that."

"Uh-huh. Tell me about this Kingsley dude. Young? Handsome? Rich?"

"Oh, for goodness' sake, Joline!" Lisa glanced nervously at the children playing on the floor. Sunny was always keenly clued in to whatever was going on. But now, intent on where Peter placed the jigsaw pieces, she was not even listening. "What has that to do with anything! I was just glad he told me to get some help. I know you don't like driving out here and I was so afraid you wouldn't come. But I've missed you, Joline, So I just crossed my fingers and dialed. And you came!"

"I was curious. So tell me. How did you manage it?"

"But you know. I told you I—"

"Yeah, yeah. I know how you got here. What I want to know is how you moved up from cleaning woman to…'' Joline rolled her eyes and made a halo gesture around her head. "To the lady in charge!"

Oh, you!" Lisa glanced again at Sunny. "I'm not the—"

"You hiring me, ain't you! And, come to think about it, we better get some things straight, I don't do windows, and I don't—"

"Oh, shut up. Have you finished?" Lisa stood up. "I'll put these in the dishwasher and we can start upstairs."

"No, I ain't finished. You ain't satisfied my curiosity. Pour me another cup and tell me how you got so high and mighty you hiring help to do what you were hired to do in the first place!"

"It's not like that. He just said…oh, something about me having enough to handle. Oh, stop looking at me like that. I don't know why." She didn't know why he had seemed shocked, even mad, when he saw her scrubbing the floor. And later… "He just said I should get someone to do the heavy cleaning."

"Uh-huh."

"The thing is…he likes me to spend time with the children. You know, make sure they get proper care."

"Uh-huh."

"And…well, he doesn't like to see anyone overloaded."

"Uh-huh."

"Oh, stop sitting there, grinning like a loon." Lord! What would she think if she knew about that kiss!

"Just wondering," Joline mused.

"You're trying to make something out of nothing!" It was nothing. Light and casual, hardly felt.

So why had it burned right down to her toes! Still burned.

"You're not here to wonder," she told Joline. "Let's get going. Come on, kids. We've got to help Joline

"All right." Sunny jumped up and took Joline's hand. "I'll help you make the beds. I know how to make the sheets nice and smooth."

"Do you now!" Joline smiled down at her as they mounted the stairs. "My, my! You are going to be a big help."

"I'll show you where to put Peter's things, too. He's just four years old and…"

Sunny's continuing chatter was a welcome distraction. Joline's insinuations had rattled Lisa considerably.

As if I hadn't been rattled enough by one little stupid meaningless kiss. Which was just…well, a kind of friendly salute. Nothing. At least nothing to him, she thought, touching the spot on her forehead. Now, in fact, it seemed he purposely avoided being alone with her. Since that day, he had not lingered one night after the kids were in bed to talk or play cards, or…or anything!

Anything? Just what did you have in mind, Lisa Reynolds!

Good Lord! She was getting paranoid, or… *horny?*

Her face burned red-hot at this thought. It was certainly nothing like that. The thing was, she was just plain starved for adult companionship. Which was why she was glad this temporary situation was soon coming to an end. And why, she thought as they finished the bedrooms and Joline started on the bathrooms, she craved Joline's company more than the cleaning.

Sunny trailed after Joline. "Are you going to put on those rubber gloves?"

"I sure am. Don't like what that bleach does to my hands."

"That's what Lisa says. But she didn't used to wear them because she was in a hurry and gloves slowed her down. But now she does."

"Does wear gloves?"

"Yes. And she puts cream on her hands, too, to keep them nice and smooth."

"Oh..." The signifying implication in that one syllable carried all the way to the bedroom where Lisa, folding clothes, had heard every word. She gave Peter's shorts an indignant shake.

Joline's company was one thing. Her stupid insinuations were quite another!

It was blazing hot in Sacramento when Lisa visited her grandparents that last Sunday in June. Nice and cool in the retirement facility, but the drive back was a trial. The air conditioner in her car wasn't working, the traffic heavy and the weather in the Bay Area unusually hot and humid.

Nothing could have been more welcome than Sunny's greeting. "We're swimming, Lisa! Come on." Welcome for two reasons, she thought. One, she was glad to see that Tray enjoyed the kids when left alone with them. Two, she was hot and sweaty and eager to plunge into the pool herself.

Two minutes later, Lisa was cavorting with them. Both the children were pretty good swimmers, though Peter preferred to traverse the pool on Tray's back. Tray didn't seem to mind. Lisa was impressed at how patient and protective he was with both kids. She noticed how his eyes constantly followed their every move. She also noticed how handsome he looked in his black shorts, his long slim muscular legs, his...

Oh, for Pete's sake! She should be watching the children, not Tray! "Let's play basketball, girls against boys!" she shouted, tossing the ball, and just missing the hoop, suspended at one end of the pool. There was a chorus of agreement, and they were engaged in a rollicking, though heavily mismatched, game when the doorbell sounded.

"I'll get it," Lisa said, grabbing a towel. "It's probably the paperboy." She couldn't think of anyone else who would be calling. The boys from next door would have come to the back gate. She opened the door, unprepared for the vision before her. The woman was exquisite. Hair so golden-blond it might have served as a Clairol commercial glinted against the setting sun, and framed a hauntingly lovely face. Her skin was flawless, as pale and smooth as marble, her patrician nose had a slight tilt, and her mouth was a perfect cupid's bow. Her eyes of vivid green were matched by the sleek sundress that clung to her bodice and billowed over long slender legs.

The vision seemed equally unprepared for Lisa. "Is this...?" She blinked. Then stepped back to examine the house number. "Mr. Kingsley's residence? Tray Kingsley?"

"Yes." Lisa opened the door wider. "Come in. He's... I'll get him," she said, and led her to a seat in the living room. Unaware that the woman followed, she went onto the patio, and called, "Tray! There's someone here to see you."

Tray was not to be distracted. He was watching Peter, who, following his instructions, was about to toss the ball toward the hoop, three feet away. When the ball slipped neatly through the hoop, Lisa's cheers joined the others. "Good shot! Peter, that was great!"

Tray turned to Lisa. "He's really getting good, isn't he?"

"Yes, he is. He...oh!" She had almost bumped into the visitor, whom, in the excitement, she had forgotten. "Tray, someone is here to—"

But Tray had seen her. "Chase! You're here." He climbed from the pool, bringing the children with him. "Grab your towels and get yourself dry," he said and, swinging a towel over his own shoulders, he stepped onto the patio. "It's good to see you, Chase. When did you get in? I didn't expect you today."

"Obviously."

The word sounded cold, like a rebuke. Tray didn't seem to notice. "You said you'd be here about the middle of the week, and I had planned to meet you, but—"

"I wanted to surprise you. I can see that I did."

"You certainly did. And came all the way out here. How did you—?"

"By cab of course. I thought you might spare time from your activities to drive me back."

"Of course. I'm glad you're here. Lisa, I'd like you to meet Chase Lawson. Chase, this is Lisa Reynolds."

"Oh?" The nose seemed to tilt higher as she nodded. "Your housekeeper," she said, emphasis on the last word.

I don't like you either, Lisa thought, returning her nod.

Tray, an arm around each child, pulled them forward. "This is Sunny and this is Peter, Chase. Say hello to Ms. Lawson, kids."

"Hello," Sunny said. Peter clung to Tray's leg.

"And hello to you." Chase Lawson bent toward them. "I'm so happy to see you. Tray has been telling me all about you, and I've come to take care of you."

"Lisa takes care of us," Sunny said. "We don't need nannies anymore."

"Oh, I'm not a nanny! But I've been looking for a nice home for—"

Lisa and Tray spoke simultaneously, cutting her off.

"Come on. We'd better shower and dress," Lisa took both children by the hand to pull them inside.

"What about a drink?" Tray was saying to Chase.

"That would be nice. Ice tea, I think." She deliberately turned to Lisa. "With lemon and mint if you have it, and lots of ice. Sit down, Tray," she said, seating herself at the poolside table. "We need to talk."

"Of course," he said. "As soon as I get your tea."

Upstairs, as soon as the kids were dressed, Lisa pulled out their favorite books, determined to keep them occupied and away from the visitor. As soon as she began to read, both children dozed off. A bit late for napping, but by the time they awakened, Tray and the Lawson woman would be gone, and that would be good. She didn't want that woman anywhere near Sunny and Peter.

What had she meant, anyway? "I have come to take care of you." She had added, or started to add something even more disturbing, "I'm going to find a nice home for you."

The fear that had nagged Lisa from the first hit her more forcibly. Did Tray really mean to dump his own children?

He had said so. Many times. "This is temporary." "When the children are permanently settled."

It was, after all, none of her business, and she had never questioned nor discussed it with him. But she was reminded of an old saying. "What you do speaks so loud that I can't hear what you say." That was true. His actions were so attentive, so caring In spite of what he said, she had begun to feel that he would always want them with him.

But now...

That woman! He had been expecting her, had planned to meet her. And that demanding voice was the same she had heard so often on the phone. "I'd like to speak to Tray Kingsley." Those phone conversations had gone on forever it seemed.

Oh, yes, they were pretty cozy. She had planned a wonderful Sunday afternoon surprise for him, and had been darn upset when she found him delightfully occupied with his kids.

Had they marriage plans in mind as soon as they got rid of the children!

Stop it, Lisa Reynolds! Your imagination is running riot.

Well, they *were* pretty darn cozy. She was beautiful. And Tray was a man.

Was there a ring, an engagement ring on her finger?

Forgot to look. Not that that means anything. And why can't I turn off all these predictions that are coming straight out of my head!

It's as if I'm jealous or some stupid thing like that, which I certainly am not!

She heard Tray coming up the stairs, and lay back on her bed, pretending sleep. She supposed he had showered and dressed before he came to tap lightly on her door.

She spoke, as if stifling a yawn. "Yes.?"

"I'm taking Miss Lawson into town. Don't wait dinner for me. I'll probably grab something there."

Probably grab more than dinner, she thought as she called a casual, "Okay," as if she didn't give a darn which, of course, she didn't. All that concerned her was what was going to happen to the children.

But, as she watched him pull out of the driveway, that woman by his side, she felt a surge of pure rage that had nothing to do with the children.

CHAPTER ELEVEN

"You're staying at the Sheraton?" Tray asked as he pulled onto the freeway.

"You know that's where I always stay!"

"Right." Tray responded automatically, too engrossed in his discomfort to notice her sharp tone. Hell of a time to be all suited up with coat and tie, and out in this heat and heavy traffic. It had been cool and pleasant in the pool with Lisa and the kids. He smiled, thinking of Peter, kicking his little legs to keep himself afloat and tossing that ball smack into the middle—

"All right, Tray. Tell me what's going on!"

"Oh, you know me. Business as usual."

"I certainly do know you, and I'm not talking about business!"

There was no mistaking the belligerence this time. Tray, his eye on the rearview mirror, frowned. That van was right on his tail! "What are you talking about, Chase."

"I'm talking about that Lisa person. She's no more a housekeeper than I am."

"Well..."

"She's no cleaning lady, either."

"Not usually. But she got in a bit of a jam and took it on. She's really a—"

"You don't have to tell me what she really is. I can see. Standing there in that little strip of a bikini

122

showing off every inch of her bare skin and that comehither look in those big eyes! Oh, yes, I knew what she was the minute I saw her!''

"Now, wait a minute, Chase. She's not..." Damn, that van's too close." He sped up and pulled around the blue car in front of them, into the other lane. A big mistake. Or it didn't make any difference. All lanes were slowing down. Some trouble ahead.

"I understand now why you have been avoiding me.''

"Come on, Chase. I'm in California and you're in New York," he said, skirting the issue. He recalled that one of the reasons the move to California had been attractive was that she had been closing in on him...just like this traffic was closing in on them right now. "I've been fully absorbed with these mergers, and—''

"Just stop it, Tray Kingsley! You've been back to New York almost every week and I've seen you only once. Briefly at that. And you've not been bogged down with business. It's that woman!''

"Damn it, Chase! What do you take me for! I've never *ever* laid a hand on any woman in my employ.'' His voice rose. The accusation stung. Especially since it had taken all the restraint he could muster to keep his hands off Lisa. "I wouldn't take that kind of advantage.''

Chase seemed to sense his irritation and, as she had a way of doing, switched tactics immediately. "Oh, Tray, darling, I'm not accusing you.'' Chase sounded both apologetic and relieved. "It's just that you're such a loving, caring, darling...patsy! I know how others can take advantage of you. Like this Kathy person, dumping her kids on you. I don't like your being used.'' Chase's hand gently caressed his thigh.

He shifted in his seat. The traffic was now at a standstill and he felt more closed in than ever. ''I don't mind. I'm glad to do this for Kathy. And for my mother,'' he added. ''This is what she would have done.''

''I understand how you feel. But...'' She gave him a wary glance. ''I worry about you, Tray. Too much sentiment, too much caring. People prey on that. Like this woman who turns herself into a housekeeper just to get near you.''

''That's not true. She didn't even know me. I told you. The lady next door sent her cleaning lady to do my house. As a matter of fact, she'd been cleaning the house for three weeks before I even saw her.'' He hesitated, remembering he had seen her in an elevator. Had kissed her. Had felt...

''But she saw you, sweetie! And sized up the situation.''

''That was easy. Anybody could see I needed help.''

''What she saw was how you could help her.''

''Well, yes. The arrangement was mutually beneficial.'' He tried to remember. Had he told Chase how he happened to hire her?

''I bet it was she who suggested it?''

''Yes, but—''

''Then she moved in, took over and made things very, very comfortable, didn't she.''

''Certainly more comfortable than it had been.''

"Fixed delicious meals or little snacks for you when you came in late?"

"Well..."

"Oh, you don't have to tell me. I know the games such women play."

"Look, Chase, Lisa isn't playing games. She is just doing a darn good job of keeping house and taking care of the kids. And that's all she's doing!"

"Oh? Do you mean she's not being very charming, and very available for a little companionship whenever you're there?"

"Well..." He thought of the gin rummy games, the talks about business and—

"And you don't have to tell me how she looks. I've seen her. That swimsuit was designed to drive a man crazy. And, believe me, that's what that Lisa person is trying to do to you!"

It didn't take a swimsuit. He thought of that rumpled shirt and the cutoffs when she'd been scrubbing. That kiss. God, he'd wanted to...

Well, he hadn't. And he had been careful not to be alone with her since then.

Once she was out of his employ...

"Don't worry. She'll soon be out of your hair! I'll see to that." She gave his leg a possessive squeeze. "Now, where are you going to take me for dinner? That is, if we ever get out of this horrible traffic snarl."

Lisa couldn't sleep. She couldn't understand it. She had had a late dinner, kept the children up long past their bedtime and had herself watched a late movie.

She couldn't remember what the movie was about.

Her mind had been on Chase Lawson. Lawson! Of course. Lawson Enterprises. She was the boss's daughter, or sister, or... Anyway of the Lawson family, and evidently part of the company. No wonder she looked at Tray as if she owned him!

Ha! That proprietary air had nothing to do with business!

Well, he had certainly jumped to heel. "Don't wait dinner for me. I'll probably grab something—"

She glanced at her bedside clock. Almost two and he still hadn't returned.

Oh, for goodness' sake, Lisa Reynolds, what's it to you how late he comes in or how gorgeous the woman he's with or...anything!

It's not your business either that he has a six o'clock flight to the Philippines in the morning, or whether he has packed, or...

Good Lord! You're thinking like a wife. A jealous fishwife at that!

Maybe in the ten days he's away, you'll remember that you're just his employee. Temporary.

She'd get her résumé off to that L.A. company first thing in the morning.

Right now she was going to sleep!

She punched her pillow and managed to do just that. She didn't hear him when he returned, or when he left early in the morning. His hastily scrawled note, giving his direction and a promise to call did not relieve a deep sense of loss.

She kept up a cheerful front as she dealt with the children, and went about her chores. She had just put the children down for their midday nap, and was stacking the luncheon dishes when the doorbell sounded.

Again she was surprised to see the vision. Smart and chic this time. But just as seductive: long, slender legs tapering provocatively into plain black pumps, her figure subtly enhanced beneath the black linen sheath. The gorgeous golden hair was piled high on her head. Her lashes were a little darker and... Were they naturally that long and thick?

The green eyes flashed. "Aren't you going to let me in?"

"Oh! Of course. I'm sorry." Lisa stepped back to admit her. "Do come in. I thought..." Didn't she have his itinerary? "Tray...Mr. Kingsley isn't here. He's—"

"I know where he is. I came to see you." Chase Lawson spoke to Lisa, but she was surveying the house. She stepped briskly into the living room and gave it a quick inspection before turning to Lisa. "You do seem to keep things tidy. That's good."

"Thank you," Lisa muttered through tight lips.

The woman didn't seem to hear her. She had moved through the dining room and into the kitchen. Lisa, feeling invaded, followed.

"Yes." Chase gave a satisfactory glance around the kitchen, then she turned to inspect Lisa. "You don't wear a uniform?"

"Uniform?"

"I can see that you don't. And those shorts will certainly give the wrong impression. Poor Tray. He never thinks of such details." She sighed. "No matter. I'm here now. I promised him I'd take care of everything, and I will. I'll get you something decent to wear. It certainly wouldn't do to present you barefoot and in those worn-out cutoffs.''

"Present me?"

"As a proper care taker. Dear me, I can see Tray hasn't told you that prospective parents will be coming in to view the children. He's anxious to get them settled so he and I can go on with our own lives.''

Lisa was convulsed by a wave of nausea. He was really going to desert his own children? He was so gentle and caring with them. She had hoped...

But... To please this woman he was going to marry?

Could he really be that callous? She hadn't thought... Her knees felt weak, and she stood mute, trying to take it all in.

Chase Lawson regarded her as if exasperated. "I should have thought Tray would have explained to you. But the poor man is so busy. He has left it all to me. He does want to be sure that the children are placed in a good home and that won't be easy. They are not babies. Any family who might consider adopting an older child will want to be sure he has been reared in a good environment, and... Oh, why am I bothering you with details! The point is we'll have to get cracking. I'll get you outfitted, and yes, I'd better check the children's clothes, too. They certainly looked bedraggled yesterday.''

"While swimming?" Lisa sputtered as rage swept away the nausea. "Did you expect them in starched pinafores and patent leather shoes?''

"Oh, dear. Now I've upset you, and I didn't mean to. I'm sure you've managed as well as you could

under the circumstances.'' Her smile was so con-
descending Lisa wanted to scream. ''It's just that
appearances can give the wrong impression. I mean
to have everything in order before I give Ms.
Clayton the go ahead.''

''Ms. Clayton?''

''From the Children's Service Agency. She will
be bringing in prospective adoptive families to see
the children.''

The idea was so appalling that Lisa couldn't
speak. She wanted to grab this woman by that mop
of piled-up hair and throw her out of the house.

She restrained herself. Remembered in time that
she was an employee. Tray had left this woman in
charge of his children. Apparently she thought with
irritation, that includes the house and me! All I'm
to do is follow orders.

Or walk out.

She couldn't do that. Couldn't desert the children.
Couldn't leave them totally in the care of this coldhearted woman.

The woman Tray was going to marry!

Good. He deserved the icicle.

But Sunny and Peter. Those kids…those poor
poor kids.

She was so mad she could hardly speak to Tray
when he phoned. She murmured monosyllabic an-
swers to his questions. ''Yes. No. We're fine.''

He seemed puzzled, and interpreted her cryptic
response as a bad connection. ''Just want you to
know I may be here longer than expected,'' he said.
''Here's my direction. If you need me…''

She didn't even mention Chase Lawson. She

wouldn't give him the satisfaction of knowing that his future wife was on the ball, taking care of all those details he was too busy to take care of himself! Following his instructions!

She felt as helpless as the children as she watched Ms. Lawson arrange things to her satisfaction. She felt even more helpless in the days that followed, her anger increasing each time the prim Ms. Clayton brought a couple, even a few singles to "inspect" the children.

She tried to protect, or at least prepare the children. "We're going to have visitors today. We must be very nice to them. And we must look nice. Would you like to wear this pretty new dress?"

It did occur to her that she might dress them in rags and tell them to be obnoxious.

Difficult. They were not obnoxious children. Sunny was maybe just a little too precocious at times, and Peter too timid, and forever making a mess. But, in truth, they were just average.

No, not average! They were the sweetest, best behaved, most delightful, loving kids she had ever encountered, and what was happening to them was breaking her heart! She wanted to scream when she heard one woman say to Ms. Clayton. "Oh, we'd love to have that darling boy! The girl is a bit too old and a little set in her ways I think. But yes, we'd certainly want the boy. What's his name?"

Ms. Clayton's reply was hesitant. "We hadn't discussed separating the children. I'll have to check with Ms. Lawson."

Check with Ms. Lawson! Lisa, listening near the door, wanted to spit out that they weren't her children. They're his! She wanted to tell them that Tray would never allow the children to be separated and he surely would not release Peter to this horrible woman who didn't know his name or about his nightmares! Tray wouldn't do that!

Would he? The thought was chilling.

At least the children were out of hearing. At a signal from Ms. Clayton, Lisa had ushered them outside before the discussion began.

This was not always the case. At times a prospective adoptive parent got too exuberant to be restrained by Ms. Clayton. Like the motherly woman who knelt before Sunny, took her hand and asked, "How would you and your little brother like to come and live with us?"

"We couldn't," Sunny said. "We have to stay with Tray."

The woman had made extravagant promises of a pretty little room of her own and lots of dolls, and wouldn't Peter like to have a dog. "Maybe," she suggested, "if he knew we were going to take very good care of you, it would be all right with Tray."

"No. He needs us. We have to take care of him." Sunny seemed to catch the woman's skeptical smile, and quickly added, "He says he wouldn't know what to do if I didn't find his car keys and bring him his briefcase so he wouldn't forget it. He needs Peter, too." Her confidence slipping, she appealed to Lisa. "He does need us, doesn't he?"

"Yes, he does. And I need you right now," Lisa responded. Muttering a "pardon us" to the couple, she hurried out with both children. She couldn't take much more of this.

It was getting to the children to, she realized when Sunny asked, "Are we settled, Lisa?"

The question gave her a jolt, coming out of the blue just like that. "Well, I, er... Why?"

"Because we couldn't have a dog in the hotel, but Tray said we could when we got settled. Are we settled? Can I ask him now?"

"Let's..." She cleared her throat, but it still came out in a choked whisper. "Let's wait and see. When..." She wouldn't say, "When he gets back." She didn't know what arrangements the officious Ms. Lawson was making with that Clayton woman, didn't know what would happen when he got back.

She did know one thing. She herself had a few things to say to him. It was time for her to walk out. But not before she told him what a weasel he was for doing what he was doing to his own flesh and blood!

They were just sitting down to lunch on Tuesday when his car came up the driveway.

"Tray's home," Sunny cried, jumping up. She and Peter ran out to meet him, "helped" with his luggage and were climbing all over him as soon as he entered the house.

As Lisa watched, her heart gave a crazy flutter. He was so handsome, so vitally alive! He looked as if he had spent more time on a beach than in a stuffy office. His skin was a deeper tan, his hair lighter, as if bleached by the sun, and he radiated with a healthy, glowing energy. She wanted to reach out and touch...

She put a hand to her misbehaving heart as if to

stop the wild fluttering. She was glad he was too occupied to see her drooling over him!

How could she drool over a man who was tied hard and fast to another woman! A man she didn't even like.

"Would you like to see what I brought?" Tray sat in the middle of the floor, opened his suitcase and extracted the presents...a small toy train for Peter, a doll for Sunny and other trinkets. The children were delighted and curious about the toys, unlike any they had seen before. Tray was patient and relaxed as he told them about the country where he had been.

How could he? Lisa wondered, with a renewed burst of fury. How could he sit there, playing the loving, doting father, while plotting to get rid of them as quick as he possibly could!

"This is for you, Lisa." Reaching up to give her a small package, his eyes widened as if for the first time, noticing the white smock and flat white oxfords. He roared with laughter. "Lisa! What are you doing in that nanny getup?"

Sunny answered before she could. "We have to look nice. We've been having lots and lots of company."

"Oh?" His questioning gaze flew from Sunny to Lisa.

Again it was Sunny who answered. "Ms. Clayton knows lots of people and she brings them to see us. Do you know Ms. Clayton?"

"No, I don't believe I do. Who is she?"

This time Lisa broke in before Sunny could answer. "Why don't we finish lunch? After your naps you can tell him all about what we have been doing. Shall I fix a sandwich for you, Tray? Coffee? Tea?'' She led them back to the table, and switched the conversation back to Manila and kept it there until she hustled the children upstairs. Sunny was getting too old to nap, but she told her to rest with a book—out of hearing while she told Tray Kingsley what she thought of him.

Only now that she had the opportunity, she hesitated. What he did with his children was his own private affair. She shouldn't butt in.

Still, she was concerned. She wondered how to voice her concern in a nonjudgmental, diplomatic way. How to begin?

He began, as usual, coming straight to the point. ''Who is this Ms. Clayton? And lots of people? What's going on?''

As if he didn't know! ''She's the lady from the agency.''

''What agency?''

''The adoption agency. Ms. Lawson said you were anxious to have the children placed in a good home.''

''Oh, yes, I am,'' he said, as if at last beginning to understand. ''And I did ask Chase to look into it. But I came straight here. I haven't spoken with her. Did she find a good family?''

Her temper flared. ''We didn't inspect. We were inspected.''

''What do you mean?''

''I mean there were loads of families and I don't know how good they were, but they came to inspect the children. Sunny and Peter....all dressed up and told to behave. So innocent and unaware." Her eyes were filling and she fought to hold back the tears. But she couldn't hold back the fury. "How could you! How could you do this to your own children!"

"My...? Wait a minute, Lisa. You're on the wrong track."

"I know. I haven't the right. I shouldn't say anything, but..." All diplomacy deserted her. "How could you stand to have your own children paraded like a couple of pedigreed dogs before people who might consider buying."

"I'm sorry. I didn't mean it to be like that. Sit down, Lisa, and let me explain." He led her back to sit in the booth.

Lisa pushed back dirty dishes, and put her hands to her face to hide the tears.

"I...I thought you loved them"

"I do love them. But...Lisa, listen to me. Sunny and Peter are not my children."

She jerked her head up and stared at him. "What?"

"I should have told you. But to tell the truth, I didn't think about it. By the time you came along I was so muddled..." He smiled. "But you know all about that. Let me tell you how I happen to have them," he said. She listened as he gave her a detailed account from the day he received the lawyer's call until the present.

"They are not even related," she said, amazed. "In fact you hardly knew them."

"I had seen them only once. And that was a couple of years ago."

"But you didn't hesitate. You brought them back

here with you." And made them feel safe and loved, she thought.

He shrugged. "Nothing else to do."

"You could have left them with an agency there."

"No, I couldn't. Let me show you Kathy's letter," he said, and went upstairs to retrieve it.

Lisa's eyes misted again as she read the letter. That poor woman. So frightened that her children might be left alone. It was as if she had a premonition. She knew that Tray couldn't have left them with an agency. Not Tray.

"I don't know why she entrusted them to me," he said.

"I do." She touched his hand. "It was a love trust."

"Anyway, you can see why I'm anxious to place them in the right home," he said. "Chase might have gone about it in the wrong way, but she means well. I'll talk to her. She is more conversant than I about this sort of thing. At least she started a search. As you see, I have done nothing."

CHAPTER TWELVE

"HE CALLS it nothing!" Lisa said to Joline, as they cleaned the kitchen the next day. She had settled the children before the television in the den so she could talk freely. "He thinks he did nothing for them. Can you believe that?"

Joline frowned at the sink she was scouring. "Guess he thinks he oughta had 'em in a proper home by now."

"Goodness, that takes time. Think about what he has done! Here he is, a bachelor, living in a hotel, or no place really, the way he travels around. Merging, switching and dismantling whole companies, dealing with governmental regulations, and negotiating with all levels of personnel. That takes a whole lot of doing, believe me! Then, out of the blue all of a sudden he gets this call and finds himself faced with the total responsibility of two small kids he hardly knows. He must have been in shock!"

"Yeah, guess it did throw him. Him a single man."

"And... Oh, God, Joline, can't you see how Sunny and Peter must have been feeling....their mother suddenly gone, all alone and scared to death."

Joline shook her head. "Poor little tykes."

"And Tray..." Lisa's heart flooded with warmth. "He's such a loving and compassionate man. He

137

knew exactly how I felt that time when Gramps got lost. He just held me and let me cry.''

Joline gave her a searching look. ''Yeah, you told me.''

''And he knew how Sunny and Peter felt. He just scooped them up and held them close.''

''Uh-huh.''

''Lord knows he didn't have a clue what else to do.'' She smiled, thinking of his early efforts. ''He might have blundered, but he really cares about them. He told me to take off that nanny outfit. We weren't to be inspected. It was to be the other way around. He meant to inspect the families.''

''Oh?''

''I guess that's what he's doing. No couples and nobody from the agency has been here since then. He may not have known how to go about it, but somehow he has managed to make those kids feel not only loved, but safe and secure.'' And he means to keep them that way.

Joline's brow lifted. ''Seems Mr. Kingsley has gone up a peg or two in your thinking.''

''I didn't understand. I thought… Oh, never mind. I should have taken my cue from the kids. They adore him from the beginning. You should see how Peter clings to him.''

''Maybe that's what's worrying the man.''

''What do you mean?''

''He sees they may be getting too close. He ain't got no proper home for them. Leastways, this one ain't permanent. And you the only one holding it together. You know what a mess it was 'fore you took over.''

"Yes, and I only did it to get myself out of a jam."

"That ain't true. You told me yourself that you was feeling sorry for those poor kids."

"And blaming him!" Lisa said. Her cheeks grew hot with guilt. "Thinking he was a horrid deserting father. And all the while he was so loving and caring. Joline, he must be the kindest, most loving, generous person alive. And always so calm and good-natured and...well, lots of fun."

Joline turned and leaned against the counter, arms folded. "Oh?"

"And I do think he's as taken with Sunny and Peter as they are with him. He'd be the perfect father for them"

"Oh?"

"Well, no. Not if he's going to marry Chase Lawson."

"Who's she?"

"She's his boss's daughter and an iceberg if there ever was one. And all she thinks about Sunny and Peter is getting rid of them quick. So, she informed me, she and Tray can get on with their own lives!"

"You right. They better off without her." Joline moved toward the laundry room. "Better see if those things are dry."

Lisa followed. "I've been thinking." She took a towel from the dryer, shook it out, hesitated.

"Thinking?"

"Well..." She drew a deep breath, unaware that Joline had taken the towel from her and was folding it. "I could adopt the kids myself."

"Oh?"

"Singles are permitted to adopt. Ms. Clayton brought some out."

"Tough being a single mom. I know."

"I just hate to think of those darling kids having to go through another change. They do know me almost as well as they know Tray."

"I'm thinking about you. Seems to me you got enough on your plate with your grandparents."

"Oh, I didn't tell you. I got a job. A real one. A man from that firm in L.A. interviewed me over the phone last week, and hired me, just like that! He said my references were impressive. and I'll be making more than I made at CTI."

"Takes more'n a job to handle two kids, honey."

"I know that. I told him I couldn't start right away, that I had to take care of some family concerns first. I was thinking. Gramps is in a bad way. Sometimes he doesn't recognize Grandma, and it's hard on her. She goes in to see him every day. It might be good for her to be away. I could bring her with me, and she'd be there to take care of the kids. We'd still be near enough to check on Gramps. Of course she'd be away from her friends, but I think she would enjoy being with me and the children." Lisa had been talking rapidly, but now she paused, looking at Joline. "What do you think?"

"You really want to know?"

"Of course."

"Well, if I was you and I wanted to adopt those children, I'd adopt him first.

"Him? Who?"

"That kind, loving, most generous man on earth."

"You mean…? Oh, Joline I'm serious about this. Stop kidding."

"I ain't kidding. Pretty juicy setup here. If'n I was you I'd concentrate on keeping it."

"Keeping it? But I can't. This is only temporary."

I'd make it permanent. I'd have his ring on my finger 'fore the Lord got the news!"

"A ring? As in wedding?" Lisa burst out laughing. "That's ridiculous!"

Joline shrugged. "You asked me."

"I expected a sensible answer."

"And I'm talking sense. Oh, I know all about you do-it-yourself women libbers! But I thank the good Lord that when my two were little, I didn't have to get out and scuffle like I do now. My Joe saw to that." Joline, deep in her own thoughts, rubbed her hand gently over a stack of towels. "He's was a good and loving man. Wore hisself out loading freight on the dock so I could stay home with the kids. If he hadn't died…"

Lisa touched her hand. "I'm sorry, Joline. You must miss him."

"I do." Joline straightened. "But I was lucky to have him, even for a short time. We had a good life, him and me and the kids. And that's why I'm telling you I'm talking sense, child."

"There's a difference between a wife and a housekeeper."

"Not a hell of a lot."

"Oh, for goodness' sake, Joline. Joe loved you. All Tray thinks about me is how I keep this house."

"You don't know no more about men than you

did 'bout running a business. Huh! All Joe thought about was hanging around that bar gambling his money away till I showed him better things to do!''

"But I'm no... I don't..." Lisa tried to catch her breath. They were off the kids, and onto something that made her face burn. "Look, it's not like I'm in love or...or..."

"Sounds like you don't exactly hate him."

"Even if I did..." she said, valiantly trying to cling to common sense. "He's practically married to Chase Lawson."

"He say so?"

"She did."

"Huh! Don't have to be so. Some women's got a way of twisting what they say around to what they want."

"Well, it looks to me like they're pretty tight. And, anyway, what they do is no concern of mine," she said, spitting mad at the coil of pure jealousy tightening around her "I couldn't care less!"

"Care about yourself, don't you?"

"What do you mean by that?"

"I mean you got to look out for number one, child. If'n I was you, I'd twist things around to what I wanted. All right!"

"Joline! I wouldn't—"

"All right!" She held up a hand to ward off whatever Lisa was going to say. "You asked me what I thought and I told you!" Joline picked up the pile of linen and marched out. "Better get to them beds."

"Yeah. Instead of wasting time talking foolishness," Lisa said.

She wasn't one of those self-serving, conniving, manipulative strumpets who worm their way into a man's affections by...by...

How did they go about it anyway?

She tried to stop thinking about it.

But Joline had conjured up pictures she couldn't erase. Tray, the children, and she, a happy family; cavorting in the pool; playing in the park; at dinner or the dentist or... Oh, Lord, everywhere! Together. The children would be safe and happy and she... She would be with Tray!

Tray. Grinning at her over a deck of cards. Holding her, his hands tenderly caressing, his lips touching.

She swallowed, blinked. But couldn't shut off the image. Nor the feeling...the peculiar flutters of pleasure dancing through her heart, a wild erotic yearning in the pit of her stomach.

This was ridiculous! She looked around for something else to occupy her mind, something to do, but Joline had left everything in spotless order.

"Come on, kids," she said. "Let's take a swim before dinner."

The swim was refreshing. But Tray's message on the answering machine, "Having dinner out. See you later," was more stabilizing.

It changed the picture...Tray, and the vision, dining, dancing, intimately embracing in the privacy of her hotel room.

Good. It sure blotted out any other picture. She was able to concentrate on dinner, the bedtime stories, baths and bed for the children. Then she sat in the living room, trying to lose herself in a bestselling novel.

It failed to hold her interest. Was she waiting for him?

Impossible!

But if she hadn't lingered in the living room until almost midnight...

And if he hadn't looked so tired. He tossed aside his coat loosened his tie and dropped into the big chair, stretching his long legs before him. Utterly spent.

Her hands itched to smooth the tired lines from his face. She sat on them. "Long day?"

"Hard." He rubbed one eye. "Two-hour phone conference. Lawson's gone profit crazy."

"Wants to set up in the Middle East?"

"You got it."

She sighed. "More and more companies are making that move."

Tray spoke harshly as if needing to vent his frustration. "Of course I'm not against industrial expansion. Move part, not all, of the operation. We should be as concerned about raising the standard of living—and, incidentally the buying power—in depressed areas as we should be in maintaining our own fine standard. Good jobs, fair wages, benefit companies as well as employees."

She smiled. "Your innate compassion seems to mix well with your business acumen."

"What?"

"In other words, you're saying that the best way to insure profits is to invest in people."

He caught her eye and grinned. "Well, I hadn't

put it that simply but I guess you're right. Anyway, what I say doesn't seem to matter. I've talked myself hoarse, and got nowhere. Then I got this call from Chase and had to go to dinner to—'' He broke off. "How're the kids?''

"Fine,'' she said, bending her head to hide the sharp jab of pain. Tray and Chase, together.

"She wanted me to meet this woman who wants to adopt the kids.''

Her head jerked up. "What?''

"I told her it was useless. And it was. She seemed to be a loving, caring, kind and stable person. But I'm not about to let those kids go to a single, man or woman.''

"You're not?''

"Hell no! You saw the mess they were in when I was juggling between them and my job. It takes two adult to make a family, a home…at least the kind Kathy wanted for them.'' His eyes were focused on something beyond her, far away. "Kathy trusted me. I have to be fair to her. And to my mother.''

He means it, she thought. He'll never let me adopt. Now the pain was for the children. They were to be torn from the stability that had sustained them for such a short time. From both me and Tray. But… She had to say it. "They have become very attached to you, Tray.''

"I know. But I couldn't do it alone.''

She had to say it. "But if you're planning to marry…''

"Chase says it wouldn't work. That it's not fair to ask any woman to saddle herself with two children who are not even mine. I...I suppose she's right.'' He was looking hard at her, as if asking what she thought, for Pete's sake!

"She's right!'' she almost shouted as rage exploded within her. Definitely unfair to the children. Anything was better than being under the care of that iceberg.

He looked surprised. No, shocked, and absolutely devastated. Didn't he know what a selfish bitch he was marrying? She almost choked as she bit back the burning urge to tell him what was behind that beautiful face, those sparkling green eyes! Men could be so dumb!

"I see,'' he said, as if she had settled the issue. "And she's right about something else, too. I'm procrastinating. And that's not fair to the kids. I should do something and do it quickly. Chase says that I find something wrong with every couple who applies and I...I guess she's right about that, too.'' He seemed to be floundering, at a loss. "How do you know? How can you tell from a bank statement or the house they have or what they say? How do I know if Sunny will be happy or Peter feel safe? I just don't know what to do.''

He leaned back, eyes closed, pain and indecision etched on his face.

He loves them, too, she thought, her rage subsiding. She felt wretched. What right had she to judge? He was trying to please the woman he loved, make the right decision for two children he also loved, and yes, try to enforce major business decisions that would affect thousands of people. He was carrying a heavy load. She could no more stop herself than she could have stopped breathing.

She got up, stood behind his chair and allowed her itching fingers to have their way, to tenderly smooth the tired lines from his face, slip down to soothe the taut muscles of his neck and shoulders.

"That sure feels good," he said, unbuttoning his shirt.

"We can do better than this," she said. She couldn't solve his dilemma, but she could help him relax. Just as she had done for many a patient at the Sacramento Nursing Home. Wait." She went into the laundry room and took two sheets from the dryer, picked up her hand lotion from the kitchen counter and returned. "Take off your clothes," she said.

"Huh?"

She almost laughed at his expression. "Oh, for goodness' sake, I'm not going to molest you, but if you want a good massage, it's better if you strip. I won't look," she added as she spread one of the sheets on the carpet.

When he was curtained between the two sheets, she pulled the top one back and began a practiced massage of his shoulder muscles. "Not as convenient as a table, but we'll do the best we can."

"Nothing could be better than this," he said, between a satisfied groan and a chuckle. "Another accomplishment omitted from your résumé, Ms. Jack-of-all-Trades.

"Not included in the package deal, either," she said, laughing. "Extra, and double for overtime, Mr. Kingsley."

"Damn. This package deal can bankrupt me if I don't... Ouch! Yeah, right there," he said, sighing with pleasure.

"I'm pretty good, huh?" She smiled, her fingers probing deeper into the tight muscle. "Worth the extra."

"Now, wait a minute. You got a wheedling way, lady, with both your fingers and your dealing, but...how do I know you're qualified—"

"Easily supplied, sir. You'll have my certificate from the Red Cross, plus two year's service at Farmer's Nursing Home."

"You're kidding," he said, a serious note in his voice.

"Okay, it was all volunteer, but that counts, too, doesn't it?"

"You volunteered for that? Why?"

"What do you mean—why? Something wrong about it?"

He paused, then spoke quietly. "Not wrong. Just...unusual. A young girl...woman. You must have been busy with work and dates."

"Yes."

She had been busy. Having fun. It was Grandma who said it might be fun to do for somebody besides yourself. And, yes, it had given her a good feeling to see old Mrs. Smith smile. "Honey, you don't know what you do for these old bones." And Mrs. Watts. "I'll sleep tonight, something I hardly ever do."

"Interesting," he said. "Volunteering at a nursing home."

"Oh, for goodness' sake, it was just something to

do," she said, glad to feel the tension easing from his shoulders.

For a long while he was silent, only deep sighs expressing the pleasure he received from her probing fingers.

She was silent, too, liking to see him relax.

She became anything but relaxed. A strange, delicious agitation possessed her as her hands moved over his body. The intimacy, the feel of his bare skin under her touch, the taut muscles of his legs...long, slender, enticingly virile. Her hand moved upward, lingered, tenderly caressing.

"Good God! Stop. I...I can't stand it." He flipped over, pulling her on top of him, his arms tight around her.

She couldn't move. Couldn't stop the intoxicating tremors racing through her. Couldn't stop her lips from finding his, from parting to let his searching tongue find hers and his hard mouth take complete possession in a deep heart-shattering kiss.

His hand slipped beneath her blouse to cup one breast, his thumb gently teasing the nipple. She tore her blouse aside and lifted to him. He eagerly responded to the invitation, enclosing the nipple with his mouth, sending waves of pleasure rippling through her. She gave a little cry, seized by a titilating lethargic urgency to surrender to the sweet, erotic, primitive desire engulfing her. To give and to take, to possess and be possessed, to love and be loved.

She felt his passion as urgent as her own even as he whispered, "I want you."

"Yes. Oh, yes."

"I didn't want... I tried to hold off. But... God knows I can't help what you do to me."

He didn't want her! The words pricked. *I didn't want...what you do to me.*

It came back with startling clarity. Joline's words...I'd keep him.

Dear God, had she tried to do just that? The massage. An excuse?

Dear Lord! Prompted by her own desire, she had deliberately enticed him.

No! She wasn't one of those strumpets who wormed their way into a man's affections.

No, not his affections. Into his pants. For this was pure sex. Angry at herself, she moved away.

"Lisa?"

She forced a smile. "You're safe. I promised not to molest you," she said as she sped away.

CHAPTER THIRTEEN

HE STARTED after her, but got tangled in the sheet. "Damn!"

A string of curses exploded from him as he disentangled himself and stood, feeling angry, bereft...and ashamed!

What the hell was he doing? Chasing after some woman who was trying to get away from him!

He was appalled at himself. He was about to seduce a young woman in his employ. Considering the living arrangements, under his protection.

Seduce *her?*

Hell! *She* seduced him! She initiated the massage. Told him to strip!

Acting all proper and professional!

Until... Her touch. Her hands...so soft and seductive, her fingers tenderly probing, lingering. He had thought... Well, it sure looked as if she wanted what he wanted! Responded that way, too. With a surge of passion that... Hell, no other woman ever got me so out of control that I lost all sense of reason. If she hadn't left like a bat out of hell...

And why did she? We're not exactly strangers. Gotten pretty close, to tell the truth. At times I thought she might, well, not feel as strongly as I do for her, but might have some affection for me.

Thought she had some affection for the kids, too, didn't you!

That had really thrown him. He had hoped...all

right was sure that she would refute Chase's opinion about "being saddled with someone else's brats."

Well, it would be unfair to expect a woman of Lisa's capabilities to permanently assume the role of housekeeper.

Not a housekeeper. Wife and mother. Very different. He wouldn't have interfered with a career if that was what she wanted! He wanted her to be happy.

And he wanted her, even if she didn't want the kids.

Women! How could you read them!

Now he wondered if Lisa had any feelings at all for him. If he could somehow get back to being friends. Start from there.

He took the crumpled sheets back to the laundry room, picked up his clothes and went up to take a cold shower.

Lisa awoke the next morning, filled with misgivings. How could she face Tray? Even if she could manage to face him, how would he react?

She had a job. She could just leave. Immediately.

Leave Sunny and Peter?

She couldn't. Not until they were secure and happy with a good family.

So she had to face him. Now. Early this morning before he left and before the children got up. She showered, dressed and had the coffee perking when he descended the stairs.

"Come in the kitchen," she called. "I'm treating this morning."

He came in, giving her an apprehensive glance, quickly switching to the juice and Danish she had set out. But his voice was cheerful, even normal. "This is unusual."

"An apology." She concentrated on the coffee she was pouring.

"Apology?"

She sat and took a quick sip of scalding coffee. Swallowed. "I only massaged women in that nursing home and I forgot."

"Forgot?"

"About genes, male, female. Chemistry. Things getting out of hand."

"Chemistry can be powerful. I know." He looked as embarrassed as she felt.

"Forgive?"

He took the hand she extended. "If you'll forgive me."

The little exchange did clear the air a bit. At least she could continue her happy, carefree routine with the children.

Well, not quite as carefree. Although she saw no more of Chase Lawson or Ms. Clayton and her parade of prospective adoptive parents, Lisa did not know what plans, if any, had been made for Sunny and Peter.

She also saw very little of Tray. He told her Lawson had decided to move the manufacturing phase of his computer companies to the Far East. Tray was not happy with the decision, but he was to direct the procedure. He was still negotiating with the Seattle firm. If he was in town, he was out of the house early and back very late. She wondered how much business, and how much Chase Lawson, occupied his time.

She couldn't quite give up on the idea of adopting

the children herself. He knew they were attached to her. If she could persuade him that her grandmother would be with her to care for them...

But she hadn't yet convinced Grandma. When consulted, the older woman had hesitated, reluctant to leave Grandpa. Lisa was daunted by the prospect of maintaining three separate living quarters, not to mention the expense of a baby-sitter if her grandmother remained in Sacramento. But time was wasting. She couldn't delay on the L.A. job much longer, and if she took the children, arrangements had to be made. She decided to wait up for him the night before he was to leave for a board meeting in New York.

It was almost midnight when he came in, and he looked so tired. As before, she hated to approach him. It had to be done. She couldn't wait any longer.

"Come in the kitchen for a moment, won't you?" she asked.

"There's something I need to discuss with you. I won't keep you long, and I won't give you a massage," she added, laughing. It was better to joke about it. "How about a cup of my magic tea, or hot chocolate? Either will induce sleep."

"Nothing will induce sleep for me. Not with what I have to face when I get to New York."

"Oh?"

"My God!" he exclaimed as piercing screams sounded from upstairs.

She followed as he took the stairs two at a time. She had thought Peter was over those horrible nightmares, but they found him thrashing wildly, screaming his head off. Sunny was beside him, trying to shake him awake.

Lisa rushed to the other side of the bed, and cradled him in her arms. "It's all right, Peter. You're—"

"Be quiet, Peter." Tray's voice was firm and demanding.

"Peter's eyes flew open and focused on Tray. "You're here! You're here!" He tore away from Lisa and flung himself into Tray's arms. "He was after me and I couldn't find you!"

"I'm here now. It's all right." Tray talked quietly and the sobs ceased, but the boy still clung as if he'd never let him go. "I'll take him in with me," Tray said. "I don't think he'll get back to sleep otherwise."

"All right," Lisa said. "I'll take Sunny."

"No, I'm going with Peter." Sunny grabbed her bear.

Lisa watched the three disappear into Tray's room. She felt a little disheartened. Would they ever feel as close to her as they did to Tray?

Anyway, no one would understand or love them more than she. She would adopt them. She would!

If she ever got a chance to even tell somebody that she wanted to adopt, she thought as she went downstairs to clear away things and cut out lights. Tray had been so deep in business matters, she hadn't hadn't got to it tonight. He'd be gone in the morning, and away for several days.

Well, darn it, she'd call him at his New York office. She wouldn't wait another minute.

Magic tea or not, I'll not get to sleep tonight, Tray thought as he climbed into bed. Peter, who had stuck by his side every minute until he did so, climbed in with him, still clinging tightly and still wide-awake.

Sunny, who had moved herself and her bear over to make room, was also alert. "Tray, are we settled?" she asked.

"I'm comfortable," he said, though he felt as crowded as he had felt that first day on the plane with boy, girl and that cumbersome teddy bear. "Are you okay?"

"Yes. But what I mean is are we settled like you said when we were we could get a dog."

He tried to decipher what she was saying. "A dog?"

"Remember? You said we couldn't have a dog in the hotel 'cause they wouldn't let us, but we could when we were settled. Remember?"

"Oh. Yes." The memory burned. Promises, promises, that he'd made no move to keep. Had even had quite a session with Chase, told her in no uncertain terms to back off and she was the only person working on getting them settled.

Well, he didn't like the way she was going about it. Kathy hadn't wanted them just turned over to some agency

"If we had a dog, he could sleep with Peter and then maybe Peter wouldn't be so scared."

"Maybe." If they were in a good family who would understand. How could you tell by just looking at a family anyway. These kids were so innocent, so trusting. If they were abused or molested...

"Can we have a dog, Tray? Are we settled?"

She didn't try to catch him in the morning. He would be leaving so early he wouldn't have time to listen to anything. But as soon as he arrived in New York and had time to get to his apartment.

He might not go directly to his apartment. Sometimes he had a dinner meeting. Or a dinner date, she thought, wondering if Chase Lawson was back in New York or still in San Francisco.

He probably wouldn't be in his office until...

No matter. She'd just keep calling every number he left with her until she tracked him down. And no use lying in bed pondering it. She was wide-awake, as she had been most of the night. Might as well get up.

She tiptoed into Tray's room to check on the children. They didn't stir. Not surprising after last night. Poor little Peter, still so insecure. If she adopted him...

No! *When!* She meant to have them, meant to be there when Peter had a nightmare, for Sunny when... Oh, just so they would be hers to love and to cherish, she thought, smiling...even if she never had a husband!

She went down to the kitchen and made a pot of coffee. The pungent aroma of the brewing coffee seemed to make the day come alive, alerted her to get going

And I'll do just that, she decided as she poured herself a cup and sat down to think. She believed she could convince Tray if she ever got a chance to talk to him. He knew they would be safe with her, and would probably be relieved. So she would just go ahead with her own plans.

First, she would call her grandmother. Whether Grandma decided to move with her or not, she would surely come down and stay with the children for a few days. That would give her time to fly to Los Angeles, sign on at the new job and find a place to live. Check on a baby-sitter. No, a good child care facility might be better. Sunny would be in school in September. So would Peter, for a half day in kindergarten. Most schools had arrangements for after school care...for a fee.

What kind of school and what kind of care? And what kind of place could she afford? Down payments, even for a rental, were...

Suddenly she felt the weight of it all. She got out a pad and listed the estimated expense, weighed it in her mind against her meager funds.

"You didn't sing me awake!" Sunny, sleepy-eyed and still in her rumpled pajamas, wandered in, dragging her bear.

"Thought I'd let you sleep a little longer. But I'll sing to you now," Lisa said. Her arms enclosed both girl and bear, and she rocked them in her lap as she sang softly into Sunny's ear, "She's a very little girl, but she has a big bear. No matter where she goes, he's always there. He's a very big bear, but he looks kinda funny. She chewed off his ear, this girl called Sunny."

Sunny giggled. "That's a silly song."

"Oh, you think so, do you! Can you sing a better one? For Peter maybe?"

Sunny yawned. "Peter's asleep."

"Still? We'd better go up and see about him."

CHAPTER FOURTEEN

PETER was only half asleep, and was fretting a bit. Probably still dreaming, she thought.

"Wake up, lazy boy," she said, kissing his cheek. It was hot. Unusually hot. She'd better take his temperature.

She searched through all three bathrooms, but there was no thermometer in the entire house. Stupid. How could you live in a house with two children with no thermometer?

She could drive to a drugstore, but she couldn't leave the kids alone, and she didn't want to take Peter out.

Anyway, she could tell he was feverish and she knew what to do for that. She gave him a tepid bath, forced down as much juice and water as she could, even made him swallow half an aspirin, though she feared it might be too heavy a doze. No baby aspirins, either, in this temporary place!

Nothing she did helped. By midafternoon, she could tell the fever had mounted and he complained that his stomach hurt. Alarmed, Lisa phoned Mrs. Dunn next door. Did she know of a good pediatrician?

Mrs. Dunn said she had taken her boys to a Dr. Grimby. She thought he was still practicing, and gave Lisa his phone number.

Lisa dialed and listened to a litany of mechanical information. Location. Office hours.

Wednesday hours were from nine through twelve, and her heart sank. This was Wednesday, and long after twelve.

But the litany continued and she listened. There must be instructions telling you what to do when a child got sick after hours.

First she was told to have the patient's name and medical card number ready.

Well, she had a name, didn't she! She continued to listen.

If you wish a prescription refill, press one.

If you wish an appointment, press two.

On and on until she thought she might scream.

Finally there it was. If you have an emergency, press eight.

She pressed it, fuming. That should have been first. The patient could die while—

"Dr. Grimby's answering service. May I help you?"

She was so startled by a human voice that her breath caught, stifling her. When she did speak, the words tumbled out. "My..this boy…Peter. He's four and has a high fever and he keeps complaining of a stomachache, and—"

"His name and medical card number?"

"Peter Kingsley," she said, realizing she did not know Peter's last name. It had never been mentioned to her. "And he doesn't have a number. He has never—"

"He's not Dr. Grimsby's patient?"

"No, he's—"

"I'm sorry but Dr. Grimsby is unavailable for new patients."

Now Lisa was beyond control. She did scream. "Listen, this child is sick. His fever is high, and still climbing. We're new in town. I don't know any doctor. Where do I go? What can I—"

"Just a minute, lady. Calm down. Listen. If you don't have a regular doctor, I suggest you take the child to emergency.

"Where?"

"Any hospital Where are you located?"

Lisa told her.

"Good. You're near Children's." She gave her the directions.

"Thank you." Lisa replaced the phone, wondering why she hadn't thought of this herself. Well, you didn't think *emergency* just because a child had a fever. You called a doctor, and...

But this child didn't have a doctor. Not even a darn thermometer!

Mrs. Dunn said of course she'd keep Sunny, and in ten minutes Lisa was in emergency at Children's Hospital, Peter bundled in her arms.

At last a doctor. A nurse

Not that her concern was lessened. She was even more alarmed when she found his temperature had soared to 104. She held his hot little hand, talking quietly to soothe him, silently praying, while the doctor continued his examination

Finally the doctor turned to her. "I've given him something to bring the fever down, but we need to find the cause. I'm sending him upstairs for some tests."

In a ward on the eighth floor, she was subjected to a barrage of questions. Insurance? Medical records?

Certain procedures could not be administered without legal permission. She was given a paper to sign

She hesitated. Tray

"I'll have to call his guardian. I'm just the baby-sitter."

She made a person to person call to Tray, telling the operator it was an emergency, and giving her every number where he might be reached. All the while she fumed. He should have given her this kind of information, told her what to do if one of them became ill.

He was an incompetent bungler! He hardly knew what to do when they were well.

Well, she hadn't thought beyond to love and to cherish, either. What kind of parent was she going to be?

It seemed ages, but in less than five minutes, her call was returned. His rapid-fire questions revealed his concern with Peter's condition. It was some time before she could tell him what was needed.

He wasted neither words nor time. "Dr. Bradley, did you say? I'll call him and get right back to you." *Click,* the connection was broken.

She paced the floor and waited...apprehensive, praying her darn cell phone and all its gadgets would work right so his call would come through.

Her fright was short-lived. In less than a half hour, he called back, saying he had talked with administration and the doctor, and everything was arranged.

"I'll be there as soon as I can get a flight. Meanwhile, Dr. Bradley needs Peter's medical records, and I've asked Chase to bring them to the hospital."

Fury struck like a bolt of lightning! Chase Chase Lawson! *She* had the records. While I...

"Don't worry, Lisa. She'll be there in a few minutes with whatever Bradley needs."

"I'm sure she will."

He must have heard the ice in her voice. The pain. His apology came quickly. "I'm sorry, Lisa. I should have thought of this kind of emergency."

She said nothing.

"Well, I didn't. I'm sorry," he said again. "Tell Peter I'll be there soon. Tell him...oh, what about Sunny?"

"She's with Mrs. Dunn."

"Good. She's all right then."

She said nothing.

"Lisa?"

"Yes.?"

"I'm glad you're there. I'll be with you as soon as I can."

"Goodbye," she said and punched the Off button. He had entrusted Chase Lawson with the pertinent papers. Not me!

She couldn't smother the blazing anger. Couldn't stifle the hurt.

And nothing on earth could relieve the crushing anxiety. She was petrified. If anything happened to Peter...

She held tight to his hand, tried to reassure him, tried to hide her concern. When he was taken to another area for more intensive examination, she waited in the hall. Prayed.

Things could change so quickly, she thought. Yesterday she had taken them for a picnic in the park and they both were fine. They...

Sunny. She'd better check on Sunny.

"I've been waiting for your call," Mrs. Dunn said. "How is Peter?"

Lisa explained. "They're making more tests. I don't know how long I'll be."

"Well, don't worry about Sunny. She's a delight, and I'm enjoying her immensely. Stay as long as you have to."

Lisa thanked her, gave her the cell phone number and asked to speak with Sunny.

"Is Peter better?" Sunny asked.

"Much better," Lisa said, crossing her fingers.

"Tell him I'm glad he's not hurting anymore, and I'm going to help Mrs. Dunn put out some new plants and he can, too, when he gets back."

Lisa listened to the happy child anticipating happy, normal doings, and her eyes filled. "I'll tell him," she said as she rang off.

It was then that Chase Lawson arrived. Through the blur of tears, Lisa saw the trim figure in a chic linen suit, the swinging blond hair, flashing green eyes. She heard, as if from a long distance, the officious voice. "Ms. Rey... Lisa! Why didn't you call me? You know I'm in charge of these children."

"I guess I...didn't think. I..." Should she have called her? She had the necessary papers. "Everything happened so suddenly that I—"

At that moment Dr. Bradley appeared, urgency on

his face. He approached Lisa. "Ms. Reynolds, I don't want to alarm you, but Peter's condition is rather critical, and—"

"Just a minute, Doctor!" Chase broke in. "You should consult with me. I'm Chase Lawson and—"

"You shut up!" Lisa's hiss brought Chase to shocked silence, her mouth agape. Lisa's attention focused on the doctor. "Critical? You know what's wrong? What's causing the fever?"

The doctor shot a quick glance at Chase, but spoke to Lisa. "I'm still awaiting lab reports, but all symptoms point to his appendix. I may have to act quickly, and I'll need you to sign a disclaimer."

"Disclaimer?"

"Permission to operate. Necessary before I can proceed."

"I'll sign. Where..?"

"You'll do nothing of the sort." Chase, having regained both composure and speech, pushed forward. "You're the housekeeper, dearie. I'll take over from here." She turned to the doctor. "I'm acting for my fiancé, Tray Kingsley, the boy's legal guardian. He asked me to bring the medical records," she said, presenting the papers and asserting her authority.

"Thank you," Dr. Bradley said. "But I must warn you. There should be no delay if—"

"We will not be rushed," she said decisively. "I must have another opinion before I can give my consent to an operation."

Dr. Bradley was thoroughly confused and looked from one to the other. "Ladies, the little fellow is quite sick and if the appendix ruptures it will be life-threatening. My suggestion is to go and go now. I'll wait another half hour and meanwhile, I'll engage emergency procedures, which will allow me to operate without either of your consent.'' He turned and left.

Lisa had not said one word after Chase's ''acting for my fiancé, Tray Kingsley.'' But her emotional excursion had gone rampant.

Heartrending *dismay*. Her fiancé! It was true. She was acting for him!

Sizzling, scorching *rage!* How dare he give that unkind bitch such authority when he knows I've been with them. Loving and caring for them for three whole months!

Terror. Peter's life was in danger. A ruptured appendix could mean...

''You're taking too much on yourself Lisa. You are hired help, and not authorized to make major decisions for these children.''

''You are? I think you've seen them twice.''

''Oh, dear, now I'm getting you upset. I don't like to criticize, but I think you overreacted, Lisa. You don't bring a child to the hospital just because he's running a fever. And you don't rush him to surgery because a doctor's ready with a knife! There should be at least two opinions, and... Oh, never mind. I'm here now.'' Chase yawned, a dainty hand to her mouth. ''I suggest you get back to your housekeeping.''

Determination. Leave Peter at the mercy of this coldhearted witch? Never

''I'd suggest you go to hell!'' she said, and rushed to the doctor's office to sign the disclaimer.

The attendant met her at the door. "Oh, you're here. I was coming for you. Dr. Bradley wants you to sign this right away. Sit here, and read it over carefully," she said, laying the disclaimer on the desk.

Lisa sat and scanned the printed words. Her hand shook as she signed. Chase Lawson was right. She was hired help. She did not have the authority, nor the right to make such a decision. What if she were wrong? What if—?

"Dr. Bradley was relieved not to have to institute emergency proceedings We received this just a few minutes ago."

Lisa looked up. What was the woman talking about?

"Just in time. Faxed from New York. Here, take a look."

I hereby grant to Lisa Reynolds Power of Attorney to act on behalf of Chelsea and Peter Byrd. It was signed by Tray Kingsley, legal guardian, and duly notarized.

Lisa held the paper in her hand, the warmth of its message flooding through her. More than a legal document.

It was his hand upon her shoulder. Comforting. Trusting.

"Poor Tray. He didn't know what else to do…knowing my busy schedule."

Lisa turned with a start. She hadn't known Chase Lawson had followed her, and had leaned over to read the fax.

"You should have called me in the first place. Tray is in New York dealing with weighty matters

of which you can have no conception. He has no
time for this."

"He took the time," Lisa said. Quickly assessed
the situation, anticipated what was needed and acted.

"Of course. He feels responsible." She shook her
head. "Those children have been nothing but a burden since they were foisted on him. Don't call him
again! Call me."

"That won't be necessary." Lisa glanced at the
slip of paper...her right to care for Peter. "I'll be
here."

"Well, I hope you know what you're doing."
Chase glanced at her watch. "Good heavens, it's
after seven. I'm late for my dinner engagement. You
can reach me at the Sheraton after ten if you run
into trouble," she said as she rushed off.

If you run into trouble! Frightening words.
Reminding her they weren't out of the woods yet.

CHAPTER FIFTEEN

SHE hurried back to Peter. He was being readied for surgery, and was slightly sedated. But he seemed comforted by her presence. She walked beside the gurney, never releasing his hand until he was wheeled into the operating room.

She walked the hall. Scared. She thought of a sharp knife piercing his small body.

Out of her hands, yet she still felt responsible. If she had realized earlier how sick he was. She shouldn't have tried to get a doctor, should have taken him directly to emergency. Were they in time? Maybe she shouldn't have signed for surgery at all. Of—

The ring of her cell phone startled her. She fumbled with the buttons, finally answering.

"Oh, Lisa, I'm sorry to disturb you. What about Peter?" Mrs. Dunn asked. "Is he—?"

"He's in surgery. His appendix." Lisa's voice broke. "It'll be a while. I'm just…waiting."

"Oh, the poor dear. And you…now don't you worry. I'm sure he's going to be all right."

"I hope so."

"Is there a key to your house? Outside, I mean."

"No, there isn't. Do you need something?"

"It's Sunny. I've been trying to get her to bed, but she's quite frantic. She wants her bear, and I can't—"

"Oh, I'm sorry." Lisa became aware of Sunny's sobs in the background. "I should have left a key, should have thought." She had thought of nothing but Peter. How could she have forgotten Sunny? "Let me speak to her. Sunny, sweetheart," she said when the child was on the phone. "Listen to me."

But Sunny wasn't listening. This was not the stouthearted, precocious girl, clever beyond her years. Not the stalwart defender of her timid little brother. Just a helpless, defenseless, motherless child who had steeled herself against the sudden disappearance of a parent or someone close. Whose only support was the familiar fuzzy teddy bear.

The child's stuttering cries broke Lisa's heart. She wasn't crying for Lisa, or Tray, or even Peter. She only wanted the bulwark that had sustained her through the long, lonely months...her bear.

"I'll get him for you, Sunny. I'll be there in a few minutes." Sunny needed her now. And all she could do for Peter was wait.

She restored the bear to Sunny, and stayed to watch her drift to sleep. Then she returned to the house for a quick shower and change of clothes before returning to the hospital.

"Peter's in recovery," Dr. Bradley told her. "The surgery went well, and he's out of danger. He did lose a lot of blood, and was already a bit dehydrated. Must have been running a fever for some time."

Her fault. Peter had been listless the day before and she had just thought he was tired. And when he had that nightmare... "I should have realized that he was ill."

"You did, and got him to us in time." The doctor

smiled at her. "In a few days, you'll have your hands full holding him down. Right now, he's still heavily sedated, but you may look in on him if you wish."

She couldn't leave him. He might move and displace the needle, stopping the intravenous flow of the fluid he needed. He might awaken, frightened and searching for a familiar face. Nurses came and went, but Lisa stayed.

When he was taken to his room, she followed, her eyes on the needle in his tiny arm.

That was where Tray found her early the next morning. Huddled in the chair, a light blanket around her shoulders. The nurse said she had been there all night, ever watchful and close to Peter. Not a brat she was saddled with, but a boy she loves. How could I have thought otherwise, he wondered, restraining an urge to kiss her face, strained and anxious even in sleep.

He touched a light hand to the boy's pale face. Breathed a sigh of relief. As the nurse had assured him, Peter was sleeping peacefully and naturally.

His gaze went back to Lisa, the tousled hair, closed eyes, long lashes resting against flushed cheeks. Curled up in that uncomfortable chair, she looked like a weary child, and his heart went out to her. The past hours had been harder on her than on Peter. He wanted to take her in his arms and...

No! Surely not that. This was not the time.

What she needed now was simply comfort, a bit of that tender, loving care she had given to Peter. He spoke softly. "Good morning."

Her eyes flew open, and what he saw in them

made his breath catch. Pleasure? No, profound relief. Or something deeper?

"You're here!" She wrapped her arms around his waist, and held on.

He smiled. Whatever it was, he liked it. He buried his face in her sweet-smelling hair and pulled her closer, gently caressing, loving the feel of her soft body pressing into him. "Lisa, I—" He stopped, alarmed. She was crying. "What's wrong?"

Her head shook against his chest.

"N...nothing. It's just...Peter's all right, and you're here," she muttered through the tears spilling onto his shirt.

"So why are you crying?"

"I...I don't know."

"I do," he said. So worried, and so alone. "You've had a rough time, haven't you?"

"I was scared."

"I know." He tucked a tendril of hair behind her ear. "But it's all over now. Just relax."

"I didn't even have a thermometer."

"Yet you managed, didn't you? Beautifully. Thank God you were here. I—" He broke off, as a nurse entered, and Lisa pulled away from him.

The nurse nodded to them, and moved to administer to Peter. "Normal pulse and temperature," she told them. "And you're feeling better, aren't you, little fellow?"

Peter's sleep-filled eyes focused on Tray. "You came back!"

"You didn't think I'd let you be sick all by yourself, did you!"

"You were gone," Peter said, "and I hurted."

"But you were a brave little guy, and I'm mighty proud of you," Tray said as he bent to kiss him. "I'm here now, and you're going to be fine. That is, if you're a good boy and do just what the doctor tells you."

"And right now, we'll have a bath so we can be ready for the doctor," the nurse said.

After assuring Peter that he would not be far away," Tray turned to Lisa. "I think it's time to take care of you. When did you last have something to eat?"

She looked as if trying to remember. "I'm not sure. Coffee. I had coffee yesterday morning. Goodness, seems like that was years ago. I did go down to the coffee shop. I don't know when, but I couldn't seem to swallow anything."

"We're going to remedy that right now." He led her down the hall to the elevator. He heard her sigh and was reminded of her phobia. He turned to her.

She was staring at the Down signal he had just pushed. "I hate buttons," she said.

"Buttons?"

"You know...if you want this, press that, and if you want that, press this."

"Oh." He wondered what brought that up, but dismissed the thought when the elevator slid to a stop before them. He slipped a protective arm around her shoulder, willing her not to panic.

"I think I'll send her a present," she said.

She had stepped in complacently, her mind evidently on something else. If he kept her talking... "A present? To whom?"

"I don't know her name. But her voice... It was

such a relief to hear it. A real person to talk to and ask things. And she was so nice.''

When they stepped onto the cafeteria floor, she was still explaining that the nice person at the doctor's answering service had told her exactly what to do and where to go. ''I am going to find out who she is and send her—''

''Just a minute,'' he said, stopping. Perhaps he shouldn't mention it, but he had to know. ''You've gotten over your fear?''

''Fear?''

''Of elevators?''

She stood perfectly still, a stunned expression on her face. ''I forgot!'' She whirled to look at the elevator. ''I took Peter up. Once…maybe twice, down to the coffee shop. Then when I went to see about Sunny…'' She shook her head, clearly amazed. ''Up and down all those times, and I never even thought about it.''

He chuckled. She had been too worried about his children to be afraid for herself.

His children! What the devil was he thinking!

She was thinking of elevators. Was she really over her fear? Something good, they say, comes out of everything. But maybe it was just temporary. ''Do you think—'' She stopped. He seemed preoccupied, clearly having forgotten her silly phobia. She forgot it, too, as she breathed in the appetizing aromas drifting from the restaurant grill.

A few minutes later, she closed her eyes and sighed. ''This is positively the best breakfast I've ever tasted.''

He smiled. "Could it be that you're hungry?"

"Could be." Last night she had sat in the same spot, and hadn't been able to swallow anything. "Or maybe," she said, almost to herself, "it takes a bad jolt to make you really appreciate the plain, ordinary good things you take for granted." Stuffing herself with bacon and eggs, sitting across from him, watching him laugh about Chelsea's bear, and...

No! There was nothing ordinary about Tray, and never could she take him for granted. Just to be with him, to watch his eyes crinkle in that wholehearted grin, to... Dear God, when she looked up and saw him this morning, it was as if her world had suddenly righted itself. She had nestled into his secure, solid warmth as if...as if she belonged there!

What must he think!

Still. He hadn't pulled away, had he? He just...

"Darling! Here you are."

Lisa's head jerked up. Chase Lawson was sliding into the booth close to Tray. She kissed him on the cheek, bit into a slice of bacon from his plate and smiled up at him. "I knew you'd be here when Daddy told me about the blowup you had with him yesterday. He said you just took off for the airport, and... Oh, Tray, you shouldn't get upset with Daddy. You know how he is."

"I wasn't upset with him. I needed to be here."

"No, you didn't. You knew I was here. I brought those medical records over right away, just like you asked. And the boy is fine. I just talked to the doctor. Now, you listen to me, Tray. I don't like your fighting with Daddy, and I know he doesn't want to lose you. I'll go back with you, and we can talk with him together and smooth things over. We can take that 6:10 flight tonight and be in New York early in the morning."

Lisa stood up.

Tray reached toward her. "Where are you going?" You haven't finished your breakfast."

"I...yes, I have. I..." She couldn't eat another bite. "And I want to talk to Dr. Bradley before he leaves." Before he could stop her, she was out of the restaurant and racing toward the elevator.

CHAPTER SIXTEEN

SHE ran, but she couldn't escape the image of Chase Lawson snuggling up to Tray. Rage spiraled through her, a roiling tornado, disturbing every nerve it touched.

That woman! Kissing his cheek, sampling food from his plate, as if she had a special right to...

Reality hit like a jabbing needle. Chase Lawson did have every right.

The pain was so intense she wanted to cry.

She wanted to run and hide. This morning... How could she have thrown herself at him like... Well, not exactly like hired help!

The elevator door slid open, and she stepped out. Stopped. Looked back.

She had ridden up. Alone. As calmly as those people loading it now, not giving it a thought.

She was cured! She gave a wry chuckle. At least when she had something more pressing to worry about...like being in love with a man who loved someone else.

No, she told herself, this was not a temporary cure. Never again would she worry that something bad would happen.

Nor would she cry when it did. In time, it would fade into the past, forgotten. Tray's one-sided grin, the way it felt to be in his arms, the hurt.

The Bible said, ''Whatever things are good, think

on these things.'' And so she would. She walked down the hall, her mind concentrated on Peter's being well, her new job, and the two delightful children who would soon be hers.

''Hi, Lisa,'' Peter, said, hardly glancing at her. The IV. had been removed, and he was propped against his pillow, happily engrossed in cartoons on the television above his bed.

She smiled. It was possible. One could forget.

She kissed Peter and went to find Dr. Bradley. He assured her that Peter was on the mend, and would probably be dismissed from the hospital in a couple of days. She would give him another week, she thought, before she left him to check on her Los Angeles job. Better call personnel now, though, and set up an appointment. Call Grandma to see if she could stay with the kids.

The kids! Surely Tray would understand that she must keep them. ''I'll talk to him right away, she thought as she returned to Peter's room.

Peter was asleep, and Tray sat beside his bed, reading a newspaper.

Again she felt the urge to run and hide. Could he forget how she had flung herself into his arms?

''I wondered where you were,'' he said, laying aside the newspaper.

''I talked with Dr. Bradley.'' She glanced around. No sign of Chase Lawson. ''He says Peter should be able to go home in a couple of days.''

''Good.'' He stood his hand on the back of his chair. ''Sit here.''

Now. Time to talk to him about the children.

She couldn't. Couldn't stay another minute in this

little room with him. One day it would be forgotten. But not now. The humiliation, the pain, were still there—closing in, choking her. "I better go," she said. "Sunny."

He paused in the act of pulling out another chair. "She's at Mrs. Dunn's?"

"Yes. I...I don't like to impose."

"Sit down. You've done enough running. I'll check on her."

She didn't protest. Just so she didn't have to face him. Not yet.

Maybe, by the time he returned, she'd be able to breathe.

He returned shortly after noon, bringing Sunny with him.

"I'm glad you're not hurting anymore," Sunny said, her head close to Peter's as she stood by his bed. "And we've got a big surprise for you, only we can't get it until you come home because Tray says... Peter, wake up. I want to tell you—"

"Wait, Sunny." Lisa took her hand. "Peter needs to rest now. The next time you come he will be awake and you can tell him about the surprise." She turned to Tray. "He's just had a sedative."

He nodded. "We'd better let him sleep, Sunny. That way he'll get well quicker." It took some time to convince her, but when he mentioned Hamburger Circus, she agreed to leave.

"I think the nurses can handle Peter," he told Lisa. "I know you're tired. We came in a cab, so I could drive you back in your car."

She wished he wouldn't be so solicitous. She needed to be alone.

"I promised Sunny lunch," he said when they were in the car. "You didn't eat much breakfast. Can you stand Hamburger Circus? It's a bit noisy."

"That's fine." Maybe the noise would block out all thought.

It didn't. How could she stop thinking about him when he was right there before her, his dark eyes alight with laughter as he joked with Sunny. He was good with the children. They will miss him.

So would she. Painful to think how much she would miss his gruff, deep-throated laugh when he won at gin or bested her in one of their bantering arguments. Never to feel his arms around her, his lips upon hers...

This was ridiculous! How could she get this maudlin over a man she had known only two... well, almost three months! She couldn't be in love with him!

"Lisa, want to hear about Peter's surprise?" Sunny asked as she bit into a juicy hamburger.

"Indeed I do." She dabbed at Sunny's face with her napkin, getting the blob of ketchup on her own sleeve. Choked down an hysterical laugh. This was crazy. She was also in love with two messy children she hadn't known very long, either.

"It's for me, too, but it's not a surprise because I already know. We're getting a dog."

"A dog?" That was a surprise.

Sunny nodded. "Tray said we could get one as soon as we got settled, and now we are settled, and

EVA RUTLAND   181

we'll get him when Peter gets well so he can help
pick him out.''

Lisa caught only one word. Settled? With another
family before she told him of her plans to adopt?
Her questioning gaze flew to Tray.

He started to speak, but Sunny hadn't finished.
''Tray says we're settled right where we are, didn't
you, Tray?''

''Right, Miss Chatterbox.'' Tray tapped her
lightly on the head and got up to pay the bill.

Sunny rattled on and on about the kind of dog
they would get, but Lisa couldn't hear over the
pounding of her heart. Tray and Chase Lawson
would keep the children. Share the home she had
made. She fought to hold back the tears.

She was getting maudlin again! Stupid to feel this
way about a man who loved someone else.

And what made her think Chase wouldn't make
him happy? She was no iceberg when she was with
him!

Anyway, Tray was a big boy. He could take care
of himself!

But the children? Even now She could hear
Chase. ''Those children have been nothing but a
burden...''

That woman was going to have *her* children?

Never! Her mouth tightened in determination. She
had to convince Tray that he must let her have them!

She glanced at her watch. She had to talk fast.
Before he left tonight on...what had Chase said. The
6:10 flight?

Two-thirty now. He had to take them home, pick
up Chase and get out to the airport in peak traffic.

Not much time to catch him alone, she thought as they returned to the car. She didn't want to talk in front of the ever-alert Sunny.

He didn't seem to be in any hurry.

Goodness, he was stopping in the park.

"Promised I'd let Sunny feed the remains of her hamburger bun to the ducks," he explained.

She watched Sunny run ahead toward the lake. "I need to talk to you while we have the time," she said

"Sure. I want to talk to you, too. But we have plenty of time."

"Not before you leave."

"Leave?"

"Tonight. She said you'd be leaving on the 6: 10."

"*She* said," he repeated in a tone that reminded her of the way Joline had said it. "If you hadn't left so abruptly," he added, sounding angry. "You would have learned that I've no intention of smoothing things over with Daddy! Lawson and I are on a different course altogether."

"Oh." At least Chase couldn't twist him around her finger.

"As a matter of fact, I'm severing connections with Lawson altogether. I'm back on my own. Several of my old clients are eager for my services."

"Oh." How did Ms. Lawson feel about that? More important, how did she feel about his keeping the children? She glanced toward Sunny who was feeding the ducks. Out of earshot. "Have you talked with Ms. Lawson about your plans to adopt?"

"Oh, sure. I told her to stop sifting through families. No way to judge people by a couple of interviews, and... Well, Kathy trusted me to see them in the right kind of home." He picked up a small stone, tossed it. Chuckled. "Hell, what am I saying! The truth is I kinda got used to them. You know...I like having them around."

Yes, she did know. But... "That wasn't what I meant. Ms. Lawson... If you're going to marry her..."

"What!" He turned to her, a stunned expression on his face. "What the devil gave you that idea?"

"She—" She stopped, reminded of Joline's "some women's got a way of twisting what they say around to what they want." "I...I must have misunderstood," she faltered.

"That's for sure! I haven't, never did have any plans to marry Chase. If you thought so..."

She didn't hear him. She was trying to control her heart, which seemed to be skipping several beats. Still trying to digest the fact, delight in it. He wasn't going to marry Chase.

She was suddenly aware that his hands were on her shoulders and he was gently shaking her. "Answer me."

"I...I didn't hear. What did you say?"

"I asked if that upset you."

"What?"

"Your stupid impression that I was going to marry Chase."

"No. Of course not." But she knew her face was as red as a beet, and she was furious with herself. Never able to hide her feelings! "I only thought..." She wished he would release her. She couldn't look at him. "The children... If you're not planning to marry..."

"I didn't say I wasn't planning to marry. I was thinking of consolidation."

He had pulled her closer. In broad daylight, in a public park. She didn't care. Anywhere. Just to be in his arms. She looked up at him. "Consolidation?" What was he talking about?

He smiled. "You gave me the idea. I thought I might hire someone who could function in several capacities.

"Oh?"

He nodded. "Business partner." He lightly touched his lips to hers. "Housekeeper." Another kiss. "Mother." His tongue teased her lips. She stood on tiptoe, pressing closer. "Wife?"

The last was a question and she wanted to shout her yes! She couldn't. She could only cling to him, to the wonderful feel of his mouth on hers, the exhilarating sensations churning within her.

"Can we go get some more bread? The ducks are still hungry."

Lisa stepped back and looked down at Sunny who was pulling at her shirt. Wished the child a thousand miles away. Wished that she and Tray were alone and not in a public park. Wished...

Oh, for goodness' sake! What kind of mother was she going to be! "Maybe another day. But not today," she said to Sunny. "We have too much to do." What did they have to do? She couldn't think. She took Sunny's hand and started to walk back to the car.

"You didn't answer me." Tray took Sunny's

other hand, and walked with them. "Do you want the job?"

She felt a little giddy, but managed to answer. "You didn't mention compensation."

"Oh, how could I forget such an important item! Well, shall we negotiate?" He was grinning, that teasing, lopsided grin.

"Perhaps. What are you offering?"

His eyes held hers. "What about all my worldly possessions, all the love in my heart, forsaking all others...that sort of thing."

"Sounds adequate." She tried to keep it light, but a lump formed in her throat. "But it is a heavy load. Will there be time to...to carry out all those duties?" To be alone with him, to hold, caress and cherish, to—

"There will be time for everything," he said. "Trust me."

She knew that she could. It was a love trust.

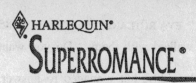

HARLEQUIN®
SUPERROMANCE®

You are now entering

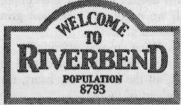

WELCOME TO RIVERBEND

POPULATION 8793

Riverbend...the kind of place where everyone knows your name—and your business. Riverbend...home of the River Rats—a group of small-town sons and daughters who've been friends since high school.

The Rats are all grown up now. Living their lives and learning that some days are good and some days aren't—and that you can get through anything as long as you have your friends.

Starting in July 2000, Harlequin Superromance brings you Riverbend—six books about the River Rats and the Midwest town they live in.

BIRTHRIGHT by Judith Arnold (July 2000)
THAT SUMMER THING by Pamela Bauer (August 2000)
HOMECOMING by Laura Abbot (September 2000)
LAST-MINUTE MARRIAGE by Marisa Carroll (October 2000)
A CHRISTMAS LEGACY by Kathryn Shay (November 2000)

Available wherever Harlequin books are sold.

HARLEQUIN®
Makes any time special ™

Visit us at www.eHarlequin.com

HSRIVER

HARLEQUIN

Duets™

Experience the "lighter side of love"
in a Harlequin Duets™.
This unbeatable value just became
irresistible with our special introductory
price of $4.99 U.S./$5.99 CAN. for
2 Brand-New, Full-Length
Romantic Comedies.

Offer available for a limited time only.
Offer applicable only to Harlequin Duets™.
*Original cover price is $5.99 U.S./$6.99 CAN.

Visit us at www.eHarlequin.com   HDMKD

Coming this September from

HARLEQUIN®
AMERICAN ◆ ROMANCE®

You met the citizens of Cactus, Texas, in
4 Tots for 4 Texans when some matchmaking
friends decided they needed to get
the local boys hitched!

And the fun continues in

3 TOTS for TEXANS
BY JUDY CHRISTENBERRY

Don't miss...

THE $10,000,000 TEXAS WEDDING
September 2000
HAR #842

In order to claim his $10,000,000 inheritance,
Gabe Dawson had to find a groom for Katherine Peters
or else walk her down the aisle himself. But when he
tried to find the perfect man for the job, the list of
candidates narrowed down to one man—*him!*

Available at your favorite retail outlet.

HARLEQUIN®
Makes any time special ™

Visit us at www.eHarlequin.com

HARTOS2

HARLEQUIN *Presents*

THE BARONS

A Texas family you can welcome into your heart

Sandra Marton's bestselling family saga
moves to the desert when Amanda,
Jonas Baron's stepdaughter, becomes…

MISTRESS OF THE SHEIKH

Harlequin Presents® #2136
On sale October 2000

Don't miss it!

Available wherever Harlequin books are sold.

HARLEQUIN®
Makes any time special ™

Visit us a www.eHarlequin.com   HPBAR5

**Don't miss
an exciting opportunity
to save on the purchase of
Harlequin and Silhouette books!**

Buy any two Harlequin or
Silhouette books and save
$10.00 off future Harlequin
and Silhouette purchases

OR

buy any three
Harlequin or Silhouette books
and save **$20.00 off** future
Harlequin and Silhouette purchases.

*Watch for details
coming in October 2000!*

PHQ400

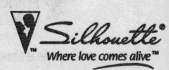

All she wants is a baby!

Popular Harlequin Romance® author,

Heather MacAllister,

invites you to share
Emily's and Freddie's baby fever!

They're best friends who've been too busy with
their careers to have babies. But now both of
them are ready to get pregnant at last....

Will their pregnancy project succeed?

Find out what happens in:

THE PATERNITY PLAN (#3625)
in October 2000

THE MOTHERHOOD CAMPAIGN (#3629)
in November 2000

*Available in October and November
wherever Harlequin books are sold.*

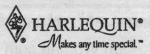

HARLEQUIN®
Makes any time special.™

Visit us at www.eHarlequin.com   HRPREG

Romance is just one click away!

love **scopes**

- ➤ Find out all about your guy in the Men of the Zodiac area.
- ➤ Get your daily horoscope.
- ➤ Take a look at our Passionscopes, Lovescopes, Birthday Scopes and more!

join Heart-to-Heart,
our interactive community

- ➤ Talk with Harlequin authors!
- ➤ Meet other readers and chat with other members.
- ➤ Join the discussion forums and post messages on our message boards.

romantic ideas

- ➤ Get scrumptious meal ideas in the Romantic Recipes area!
- ➤ Check out the Daily Love Dose to get romantic ideas and suggestions.

Visit us online at

www.eHarlequin.com

on Women.com Networks

HEUT2